HIDDEN TURNINGS

HIDDEN TURNINGS

A COLLECTION OF STORIES THROUGH TIME AND SPACE

EDITED BY

Diana Wynne Jones

GREENWILLOW BOOKS, *New York*

Library of Congress Cataloging-in-Publication Data
Hidden turnings.
Summary: A collection of twelve fantasy stories on the
theme of the supernatural touching and changing everyday life.
1. Fantastic fiction, English.   [1. Supernatural—Fiction.
2. Fantasy.   3. Short stories]   I. Jones, Diana Wynne.
PZ5.H54   1990   [Fic]   89-11742   ISBN 0-688-09163-6

Contents

Introduction

I DIDN'T at first believe that I had been asked to make a collection of new stories by authors of my choice, because the letter asking me was dated April 1. But as soon as I was convinced it was true, I at once made two decisions. First, I decided to ask for stories from all the writers I love to read myself: the people who keep me on the edge of my seat, or awake all night, or gently chuckling, or all of those things.

My second decision was that I would *not* set any theme or title for the writers. People often ask me for a story, saying, "It has to be about dragons," or "Our title is *Many Millions*." This always makes me feel utterly imprisoned, and I find I can write about anything *but* dragons or millions, or whatever. I wanted the writers to feel free to do their own thing in their own way, and, when it came to giving the collection a title, I trusted that a theme would emerge from the twelve stories, which would provide one.

You will find, in fact, that various themes run through these stories. But one thing that all of them do is lead the reader around some hidden turning of the mind into remarkable new places. Some of them have hidden turnings beyond that. Hence my title.

Diana Wynne Jones
1989

HIDDEN TURNINGS

DOUGLAS HILL

True Believer

As I BEGIN this account, my feelings—insofar as I still can claim to possess such luxuries—are unexpectedly mixed. I am surprised to find some part of me weakly regretting what I am about to do and faintly hoping that you will not believe what I am about to reveal. Yet, at the same time, slightly stronger within me is a general attitude of indifference. I know that what may befall you will not concern me in the slightest by the time it happens—for I will be, as they say, long past caring.

And the strongest feeling within me, if truth be told, is that which makes a sufferer curse those who do not suffer and seek to drag them down. I confess that I so despise and envy your untroubled ignorance that I want finally to *force* upon you the truth of my words. . . .

I HAD been holidaying alone that summer, driving and camping, drifting along scenic back roads in the countryside, loosening the stresses and tensions imposed upon me by work and play in the metropolis. On the night in question I had stopped on the borders of a sizable wood in . . . in the south of England. (I shall not make matters worse by specifying exactly where.) After setting up my little tent I went wandering deeper among the trees in the last sunshine of that late afternoon.

The sunshine and the strange silence of the woods warmed and soothed me, and made me aware of my weariness after a day's driving. As the shadows lengthened I seated myself on the soft turf, leaning back against a hummock as welcoming as a pillow. No bird twittered, no insect buzzed, no leaf stirred. As my eyes slowly closed, I felt wholly at peace.

It was an ordinary English wood, not a dark mountain in Transylvania. It was an ordinary summer evening, not Allhallows. And yet . . .

Their voices awoke me, not their arrival. So I do not know how they all came to that place—though it would have been after darkness fell, and in ways that kept them from noticing my sleeping presence nearby. Certainly they must have been gathering for some time while I slept, unaware, behind the thick bushes that screened me from the light of their fire. Their talk had no doubt begun to intrude upon my sleep. But I was roused at last to total wakefulness when one of them cried out—loudly and gleefully.

"Someone is thinking about us!"

I was raising my head to peer through a narrow gap in the bushes before the full meaning of the words struck me. And what I saw, through the foliage, in the firelight, delayed understanding further.

I remember now that at no time did I think that I was dreaming. I *knew* I was fully awake—even though I was unquestionably looking at nightmare. But shock is nature's safety cushion and it saved me then. I neither moved nor cried out. I merely looked and stared, while my muscles clamped tight like rigor mortis and horror slowly flowed, molten and searing, through my every cell.

In my very first glance they had seemed to be merely a gathering of rather oddly dressed and unappealing people. I saw that a number of them wore long, high-collared cloaks, and that the cloaked ones all seemed excessively pale, though with bloodred lips. Many more in the gathering were wearing loose, flimsy robes, usually stained and tattered, often hanging unconcernedly open. And I was startled when I saw that they wore nothing under the robes, and that others in the crowd wore—blatantly, shamelessly—nothing at all.

The entire throng displayed every variety of the human form, as any gathering of people might do. They were male and female, young and old, fit and flabby, stout and scrawny. Many of the unclothed ones were ugly enough to make me wish that they were covered—including a large proportion who were squat, stocky, and densely covered in hair. And all of them in that crowd were chattering among themselves with loose and cruel mouths, eyes that held knowledge of things unknowable, and wild laughter that even now poisons my dreams. . . .

Then I saw what else had come among those weird people in their gathering.

I saw, slinking through the firelight's shadows, huge and heavy-shouldered wolves, slanted eyes gleaming green or gold. I saw tall black goats with their yellow devil-eyes, horns shining like metal. I saw things that looked like toads or spiders, but as large as men, bulging and foul.

And beyond them, farther from the fire, I glimpsed the true shadow creatures, from the deeper reaches of manic phantasm. Half seen and wholly indescribable, shapeless shapes with many legs or none, looming tall among the trees or slithering flat along the ground, stamping with cloven hooves or spreading wings that crackled like old leather . . .

And I crouched, frozen and horrified, behind my screen of

bushes, waiting for one to stretch itself, or take flight, and look my way.

But none did. The announcement that had wakened me had also stirred that demonic throng. They were clustering around the speaker, who was one of the pale, cloaked figures, his exultant smile exposing pointed fangs as he repeated his discovery.

"There is someone thinking about us!"

"Where?" One of the robed women swirled her thick hair, a hand clawed in a gesture of desire.

"North," the discoverer said. "In a city."

He named it and specified the place. I shall not. But I remember feeling, behind my frozen numbness, a tinge of relief—that they were not talking about me.

A muscular, naked man, so hairy that he seemed fully clothed, yawned widely. "More of those stories?" he inquired. "You have been fooled that way before, Baron."

"Not this time," said the cloaked figure. "She has been reading about us, yes—but not those foolish fictions with which the simpleminded frighten themselves. This one has been reading the *truth*! And she *believes*!"

"Ah," said the woman, smiling savagely. "An occultist!"

The creatures all looked at one another, and their laughter swelled, brassy, discordant, knowing.

"And she really *believes*?" another woman asked.

"She believes," said the one they called Baron. "She is at our mercy. I shall bring her . . ."

"A moment," growled the hairy man. "I do not think, Baron, that it is your turn."

"*I* can scarcely remember," the first woman put in. "It has been so long."

"I was the one who sensed her thoughts," the Baron said icily. "It is for me to bring her."

"I say it is not," snarled the hairy man.

"It is not for either of you to say," the woman objected.

As both the Baron and the hairy man turned on her, the rest of the people began to stir and jostle, their voices rising, strident and aggressive. The hairy man crouched, flame eyed, as if to leap at a throat, and the Baron's cloak suddenly swirled around him like the wings of a giant bat. Men shouted, women shrieked, and sounds issued from the creatures in the shadows—sounds to drive men mad, sounds that human ears were not meant to hear. It seemed that I was huddled on the very threshold of hell, and that its ghastly denizens were provoking one another into an unimaginable brawl.

Then from the midst of the mass of bodies a creature hobbled into a clear space by the fire. It was an aged, naked harridan, a travesty of a woman: skinny, stooped, bandy legged, nearly bald, hairy chinned, sagging and wrinkled skin daubed with grease and filth. Leaning on a crooked stick, she stared around at the belligerent crowd—and began to laugh in a grating cackle.

"Do, then, do!" she cawed through her laughter. "Squabble among yourselves, do! Scream and growl and play the fools! Give up the whole night to such fine sport! Of course we have believers aplenty at our disposal, so we can easily overlook this one perceived tonight!"

The noise of the creatures subsided under the lash of the hag's sarcasm, and they shifted and stirred uneasily around her.

"What now?" she cackled. "Lost your taste for brawling? Some sense creeping back?" Her laughter stopped as abruptly as it had started, and I saw then that her eyes were as cold and mirthless as flakes of ice. "Fools! Do you need reminding that the people of this age have built *barriers* against our kind, in all their thoughts? Do you need me to tell you that this believer, perceived tonight, is the first to be open to us for *years*?"

The other creatures shifted again, silent now, gazing at the ground or glancing nervously at one another.

"Come, then," the hag went on briskly. "It makes no matter who goes to gather up this believer. As long as she is brought to us in good time, so that all may *play* with her awhile"—the throng murmured in hot-eyed hunger—"before we finally sacrifice her to our Master. Come, let us choose the one to send, in the proper way!"

The creatures gathered themselves eagerly as the hag raised a hand. "The parchment!" she cried.

From the shadows emerged a scaly and oozing *thing*, repulsive beyond the power of words, with a roll of parchment in its claws.

"The pin!" cried the hag.

Beside her, the youngest of the women—a breathtaking blonde girl of about fifteen—plucked from her robe a long golden pin that had been the garment's fastening and giggled lewdly as the cloth fell away from her body.

Taking the pin, the ancient hag closed her ice-chip eyes and plunged the pin into the parchment. All the people and creatures moved nearer as she peered at where the pin had struck.

"The one chosen," she said, "is Pieter."

"Pieter?" the others shouted. "Where is he? Come along, hurry yourself!"

Pieter, pushing through the throng, turned out to be a handsome youth—naked, slim, with tousled curls, his skin largely covered by a downy pelt of fair hair. But for all his good looks his heavy-browed face wore an expression that was twisted, distorted, hinting at unmeasurable depths of depravity.

"Bring her back, Pieter," called the blonde girl, giggling.

Pieter glanced around at the others. "She is still thinking of us? Believing in us?"

"Oh, yes," the Baron said, baring his fangs in another smile. "Her mind cannot deny the truth that she has read. She believes."

"She is *ours*," cackled the aged hag.

"Then I will return with her shortly," Pieter said.

He turned away—and dropped to all fours. As his hands touched the ground I saw the hair on his skin suddenly lengthen and thicken. Appalled, I watched as his face narrowed and extended, as his hands and feet shrank, as his arms and legs grew distorted. . . . The process took only a few seconds, after which I was looking at a giant gray-brown wolf standing where Pieter had been.

And it was then—as the wolf sprang silently into the darkness and away—that my shocked and tortured mind gave up its struggle, and I slumped back onto the turf in a dead faint.

———

I AWOKE, entirely alone again within those woods, which were gray with the muted daylight of an overcast morning. Deeply chilled in spirit as well as body, I lurched stiffly to my feet—noting the scattered ashes where the fire had been, but avoiding any closer examination of the site where the beings had gathered. Instead I stumbled back to my own campsite, rinsed my mouth with water, hastily packed my things, and drove back to the city like a thing pursued.

The image is apt. I knew I *was* pursued.

I recall wondering briefly if I had perhaps gone mad. But I grew sure that I had not—for, aside from the impossible sights that I had seen, my senses seemed in order and my actions under control. Equally, I remained entirely sure that I had not dreamed those terrible events. The human mind knows the difference between the fragmented and elusive memories of a dream and the sharply etched remembrance of reality. Even when that reality is, by all accepted definitions, beyond credibility.

No, I was in no doubt. The monsters, the demonic horror that I had seen, had been all too unbearably *there*, real and undeniable.

I was also in no doubt about what that horror meant for a poor, wretched woman in a northern city.

And, now, for me.

Terror seemed to have lent me a strange clarity of mind, for I hardly needed to pause to puzzle out the ghastly reality. It was more of a swift, intuitive leap that showed me the meaning behind what I had seen, behind the words I had heard.

"Someone is thinking of us," the Baron had said. As if he and, no doubt, the others could *sense* such thoughts over a considerable distance. As if someone thinking about the monsters made them *aware* of the person who held such thoughts . . . especially if that person also *believed*.

And belief, it seemed, made a person vulnerable. "She is at our mercy," the Baron had said. "She is ours," the hag had said. So there was the awful truth that I had perceived.

These legendary creatures—witches, warlocks, vampires, werewolves, demons, evil hell-spawn of every sort—do truly exist. They do prowl abroad and gather together—at night—just as the old tales say. But now, in this skeptical age, things are different.

Now the supernatural has been displaced by the scientific *un*natural. The old beliefs and fears have been relegated to the dustheaps, along with every other kind of obsolete refuse from the past. And so, in this age, skeptical humanity is no longer vulnerable to the monsters. The horrors are *powerless* against the "barriers," as the ancient hag had termed them, of our disbelief.

But, it seems, they regain their power when belief is restored.

When an individual somehow comes fully to believe in the monsters' existence, they in turn become aware of him or her. As they had become aware of that luckless woman in the northern city.

And, through that belief, the creatures renew their ability to bypass the "barriers," to grasp and assail the believer.

I did not dare try to imagine the fate of the woman whose belief in hell's horrors had been born the previous night. Instead, during that wild drive back to the city, my terror-stricken mind was fixed solely on my own plight.

I was aware that a state of shock had shielded me during the previous night, rendering my mind so numb and blank that there were no thoughts of any sort within me for the creatures to detect. And I was grimly thankful that I had been unconscious when Pieter would have brought the woman back to be the gathering's plaything and victim.

But now . . . Of course it seemed that the old tales were right when they said that the creatures were inactive by day. But, as my car sped along the highway, the day was wearing on. Night inevitably would fall. And I would no longer be in shock, or fainting. I would be entirely defenseless against the horrors.

For—heaven help me—now *I too believed*!

———

SINCE THAT evening, every night for the past many years, I have striven with desperation to blank out my thoughts, my mind, during the hours of darkness when the creatures will be gathering. Alcohol has been, of course, the easiest means— good cognac in the beginning, for I was then well off. I also learned that certain drugs, illegal and expensive, wash out the memory for some hours.

But the process of seeking oblivion in these ways, night after night, began predictably to affect my behavior during the day. Hung over, groggy and unkempt most of the time, I was increasingly unable to meet my obligations. Naturally I could not confide in anyone or explain my behavior, nor was there any kind of help that I might have sought. All too quickly I lost my job, my friends, my self-respect.

And still the terror kept me reaching for a bottle at sunset, every sunset. Today it is mostly a bottle of the cheapest and foulest stuff available. But that has not mattered—not so long as it can send me into drunken slumber before my thoughts, my belief, can betray me to that distant, demonic gathering.

So my life has become a repetitive round of drowning my mind by night and scrambling by day to find the money that I need to do it again. And on those unthinkable times when I have failed to raise the price of my protection—I can scarcely find the words to describe those nights—then I have lain awake, in a fury of desperate concentration, muttering multiplication tables or fragments of half-forgotten verse or anything that will stop my mind thinking what it must not think. And as I mutter I sweat and tremble, waiting for the slap of a leathery wing or the pad of a lupine paw in the darkness around me. . . .

It is not a life. The years have ruined me in body and mind. The most agonized prisoner in the cruelest dungeon of history has not suffered such torments as I. Yet it must go on and on—while at any moment my weakened mind might slip, think the forbidden thoughts, and expose me to the horrors.

So lately I have come to ask myself, as yet another evening draws in, could suffering and death at their hands be so much worse than the living death I have known all these years?

Such questions, such despairing considerations, have led me at last to this day. I am giving up the struggle. It is a sudden but now irrevocable decision, an impulse that has sealed my fate. And having made it, I find that I feel a measure of relief—and, also, some perverse curiosity about the imminent arrival of that which I have feared for so long.

Equally, as I said at the outset, I feel a certain spiteful satisfaction. I have spent such a long time wandering among people like you. Blithe, unaware people who have no idea that they are protected merely by the flimsy barrier of disbelief from the yawning jaws of hell. I know that my sudden decision to let go, to give myself up to death, came partly so that I could write this and give it to the world, to shatter forever that fragile shield of yours and of people like you.

For as I know very well, disbelief alters with ease into acceptance and certainty—on a one-way track that allows no returning.

So here you are. I have little time left now, for darkness is falling. My belief, contained within these pages, is also echoing in my mind, broadcasting itself to those who have the power to sense it. But there is time still for me to send this account on its way—as a story, of course, a work of fiction, which I hope will be published in the normal way of things.

Indeed, when you read it, you may simply accept it as only a story, a brief diversion, and pay it no mind. No doubt my disappearance will go equally unnoted—just one more drunken tramp gone from the streets, no one caring.

But if you can sense the rage of emotion behind this account—the cold ring of terror and truth within these words—then you may believe.

And if you do believe—you will be at their mercy.

So, now. Are you—as I did, for so long—reaching for a bottle, or a handful of pills, or mumbling numbers and verses in a hysterical need to blank out your thoughts?

Or is it too late for you? Are you instead imagining—as I am—fearsome heads being raised in a faraway forest? Eyes gleaming red in the firelight? Fangs being bared in readiness?

Are you—as I am, now—simply wondering . . . which one will come for you?

T A N I T H L E E

Ceres Passing

MY MOTHER, one of the King's twenty-six wives, was having her face creamed and massaged by a slave. It was messy, and boring to watch. Glittering insects buzzed in the colonnade. The nightly storm was crouching in the hills outside the city, and everyone felt vaguely furious about something.

The slave batted ineffectually at the insects, cream slopped on the marble. I waited.

"Tonight," my mother remarked again.

She had remarked in the same way four or five times already. It was an annoying habit of hers. Everything distracted her, the flies, the slave, the storm, everything.

"Tonight?" I asked casually. It was useless to be more pressing.

My mother selected a small, inferior cake. (The best ones went to the Favorite Wives, of whom there were five. The

12

Favorite Wives were also able to burn incense to keep the insects away.)

"Oh, how oppressive it is," said my mother, as if she had made a world-shattering discovery. She slapped the slave, who perhaps had got some cream in her eye. "Tonight, Angka," added my mother, "you are to dance in the Hall. There's someone your father wants to impress." Not impress too much, however, or it would have been the daughter of a more important wife.

"I see," I said.

"And you are not to be late again. Be there after the main courses of the feast. About the stuffed hedgehog, I should think."

The stuffed hedgehog was served, at Superior Feasts, after at least twenty dishes, but at Inferior Feasts it was twelve along. Presumably, as *I* was to dance, tonight the hedgehog would be number twelve.

I'm not a very good dancer and my father used me only on unimportant guests. They were always drunk by the moment of my arrival, so my wobbly twirls and limping efforts to resemble a "slender palm tree tossed by the wind"—as my teachers had it—were less noticeable. Perhaps they thought I was a wonderful dancer and it was the wine they had knocked back that made me look that way. Usually they were snoring by the end of my act.

"What would happen," I inquired, "if I didn't go?"

"Your father would whip you personally. You'd be scarred for life." She slapped the slave again absentmindedly.

As I got up, the storm broke.

My mother screamed as great purple birds came squawking and flapping into the room, between the pillars. Rain exploded on the floor like broken glass, and the lightning gave a huge, white wink.

"Ah!" screamed my mother. The birds rushed around us and light furnishings crashed to the floor. It would really be quite simple to murder all of us; the two courtesy guards outside the door were so used to our continual commotions that they would never take any notice. Not that they would be at their posts, or that anyone would bother to murder us, anyway. It's a marvelous status symbol to have a few murder attempts made on your life every month or so. The King's favorite Favorite Wife was always finding adders in her clothes chest or curses pinned to her bed curtains.

Birds zoomed over my head and tried to come out of the door with me, but I shut them in firmly with my mother.

In the corridor rain dappled the floor and my bare arms. Some of the tiny, furry pet animals that were everywhere in the palace sat in a puddle and gazed at me. There was no guard in sight.

=====

As I crossed the dripping greens of the gardens, lightning turned into a sizzling spear and shot downward into the city. I was sure it had struck some historic, old, useless obelisk somewhere or other. This would mean rites and religious processions for the rest of the week, in hope that the gods would intercede with furious, old, useless ancestors demanding a new, old, useless obelisk we couldn't afford to put up.

My apartments, such as they are, lie at the dank bottom of the overgrown and gloomy Sun Garden, in a sort of pagoda, once the love nook of some long-forgotten concubine. The garden leaned extra heavily on the pagoda tonight. Nevertheless, a flickering lamp welcomed me in at the porch. Inside, my elderly slave Talu was busy at her endless picking up after me, her arms full of shed clothes, her eyes full of horror at my rainy appearance.

"There's a hot bath prepared," she cried. "Into it you go at once."

Talu's only physical characteristic is her hair. It is made of iron and skewered in place by obsidian pins.

In herself, Talu has long since been trained to think of nothing but regular mealtimes, habits, baths, nourishing drinks, and so on. She therefore disapproved each time of my dancer duties, with all the frustrated anguish of the slave. She is nearly as powerless as I am.

I kicked off my sandals and dropped my clothes in the normal way as I went toward the bedchamber and bath. Talu came along behind, clucking and picking up. This was so much a ritual I did it now more to console her than anything; to my surprise, in past months, I'd become quite tidy when left to myself.

After the bath I dressed in an old silver thing and some jewelry Talu brought, looking desperate to speak and my-lips-are-sealed. When she gave up on untangling my hair with the combs and brush, Talu went off and started taking down the storm amulets she hangs out every evening, in order to hang up the other lot to protect us through the night.

"Talu," I said, "do you know who my father's guest/guests is or are?" Once I'd said it, I couldn't think why I had. It could have no possible interest for me.

Talu sniffed and said, "How should I know?"

But of course slaves know almost everything, and now it was to be a battle of wills, which poor Talu enjoyed so much, holding out, and finally giving in. So I had to go on.

"Oh, *you* know."

"I? A lowly drudge—" Et cetera.

The sunset had perished in the storm, and by now my father's dinner would be tackling course number eleven (probably an unlucky warthog).

"—But perhaps I heard the underscullion say something about a portent."

"What has a portent got to do with the guest/guests?" I said.

"It advised to be very *wary*," said Talu. "For here was One-More-Than-She-Seemed."

A single word stood out from this familiar type of injunction, which is of the sort the temples endlessly inflict on us. (Beware the failure of the evening storm, it may mean drought. Desist from wasting food, it may invoke famine. Regard the humble beggar in the refuse, he is more than he appears, for the gods now and then take human guise to test us.) The word that actually startled me was *She*.

"Do you mean the King's guest is a woman?"

Talu picked up a bracelet I had dropped to help her.

"What does a slave know?"

But now there was no more time to argue. I maliciously agreed, of course, she could know nothing, and ran out.

In the wet, haunted garden, glimmering with first night, statues and lurking ghouls with red, greedy eyes cheeped as they came alive in among the orchids. Dilapidated ghosts clutched at me on the stair. *"Angka, stop and visit me!"* mooed the haunt on the thirty-first step—which may only be wind through a split column there, but then how has it learned my name?

I thrust the door of the upper terrace shut behind me and was in the smart part of the palace. At once two guards leaped out, and finding me, as ever, Princess Number Seventeen (unlike the haunt, hardly anyone else here has troubled to take my name), they flung open great portals with bronze fitments and I came into the Hall before the King.

═══

As I'D THOUGHT, it had been warthog. Everyone was chewing with intent sullenness, or picking their teeth in obvious anxiety. Even as I entered, a cook did likewise, sweeping by me with a baked hedgehog on a platter for the high table. I felt a terrible sympathy for the hedgehog, which should have been out rattling along over some forest hillside. I had no strong emotion for any other one or thing in the Hall.

My mother was not present, along with the twenty other

non—Favorite Wives, but The Five were much in evidence, vying with each other in apparel and pets. All had the most fantastic hairstyles—both Wives and pets; sometimes the pets were even *part* of the hairstyle.

The pillars in the Hall are painted with long green and scarlet stems and end in leaves of beaten copper against the roof. Otherwise the space was full of diners and dinner and wine jars, with slaves and escaped marmosets and hamsters scrambling in all directions.

My father sat in his ebony chair with the silver lions' feet. There was nothing remarkable about him. He was just another squat man with warthog gravy in his beard.

Then I realized that there *was* something remarkable about him after all. He was extremely nervous. He was fidgeting and breathing fast, and his eyes were puffy and restless. I'd never seen him like that, although it was a mood he frequently brought on in others. I turned, to find out why.

In the guests' place, which normally is occupied only by men, sat a small bowed figure in mud brown clothes. Although a dirty-looking veil concealed her hair and most of her face, her hands were visible, and her feet were completely bare. Both hands and feet were sunburned the shade of mahogany. A trail of dusty hair came out of the veil and trickled along one shoulder. It looked the same color as her skin. Her posture was that of an exhausted slave who has just been badly beaten.

Could this be *She*?

The hedgehog, meanwhile, was being greeted with gloomy cries of praise.

The King, my father, leaned an inch or two toward the slavelike woman and said, fawningly, "Lady, here's a great delicacy of my country. Will you taste some?"

It was then I noted, from the wreckage on the tables and floor (although the area before the woman was spotless, untouched), that about nineteen dishes had been served. This was a *Superior* Feast! And for—for *her*.

And then, then, then, she lifted her head, and she looked straight past the King, and along the Hall, and into my eyes. And I saw she was a queen. No. I saw she was a goddess.

It was terribly and terrifyingly apparent, once she revealed her face—her eyes. And equally terribly and terrifyingly easy to miss if she didn't. I thought excitedly: So it's true! All that nonsense with amulets, and that stuff the priests waffle on about. And, too, it isn't, because it's not the way they tell you.

When she looked at you, you saw she wasn't mahogany but some new-minted material made on another world . . . the world of the gods. And her eyes were gold. But really she was impossible to describe. If you stare at the sun, soon all you see is a dark blot. That's all that can be left from something so bright. Words aren't enough.

Presently she spoke, in a soft, melodious voice that I knew could fill the city—perhaps the whole land, all lands—only she modulated it, just to fill the little space of the King's Hall, gently.

"King, won't your daughter dance for me?"

"Uh—*Lady*—of course! Haven't I called them all? Haven't the three best and the thirteen second-best daughters each danced, and each to complement a special dish?"

Her pure gold eyes were sad. They said, *If only*—

I'd disappointed her. It came to me dimly she'd been hoping I might be someone else . . . and incredibly, for half a second, she had seen a resemblance—but then it faded and I was only me.

I felt awful about dancing for her. It wasn't that I was frightened, for I wasn't in the least. But that was the kind of goddess she was. She scared someone like the King. He hadn't understood that you only had to accept what she was, that nothing you were could matter, that she was everything and all things, and all the numbing, roaring Might of what she was passed over like a colossal, shining cloud. It was that I felt awful about my dancing, which was so bad, and about which I hadn't troubled until now. But I'd have given anything to please her, to make her feel better for a solitary minute. And I looked a look at her, and the look said how sorry I was. And all at once—she laughed. She laughed out loud, and it was golden bells.

And something happened. There was music, but it wasn't the twanging and thumping of the King's musicians, although it must have been. She had done something to it.

I was dancing. Or, I was living something out—it was nothing I had ever felt before.

There was this dark forest, and in the forest a large clearing, a plain in the sunlight, and here I was weaving a garland. The sunlight poured around me and into me, and *I* was like the sunlight. There was a golden feel to being me. I couldn't have been ungraceful if I had tried. I ran liltingly to and fro, weaving the flowers, which seemed only more alive after I picked them, until I saw a flower that was better than all the rest. It stretched out its silken wings, which were like the purple linings of a storm and edged with crimsonlike fire. When I took hold of the flower it had a strength of its own and flirtatiously resisted me. But eventually I won. I uprooted it. The flower nestled against me and I danced with the flower, so glad to have it as it rested its head under my throat, and only at the last instant did I see it was really a snake of purple and fire— it reared back to bite at me as I stood in stony panic under the darkening sky. But before I could call my mother's name the earth opened under me, I was gone, into the darkest of all darks, under the ground.

When I had danced that, I was still not frightened, only I felt a dreadful sorrow, something also I'd never known. I knew it was hers, the sorrow of the goddess, and that she searched for me over the earth. Her golden feet passed above my head, but all I could do was tap at the shell of the ground, and she never heard.

The music had stopped. I found I was sitting on the tiles in the middle of the King's Hall and there was absolute silence. I'd never heard it so quiet there.

The people were staring at me. Even the five Favorite Wives (one with a small monkey plaited in her hair, which was eating an orange fruit all over it), even they *stared*. And, with a flicker of pride, I thought maybe I could expect a couple of halfhearted assassination attempts in the next few days. I had danced not well, but amazingly. But it had only been because the goddess had given it to me to do. The point was, most of them were so stupid they could never grasp that, they would think it was me.

The goddess was standing, and she was crying. No, she was weeping, that's the word. Or even *weeping* isn't. The tears fell from her eyes like falling stars. They left no moisture on her face. She made no noise.

She moved along the Hall as if no one else existed in it but her and me. And when she came level with me she looked at me. I wanted to touch her, but, instead, she put her hand on my head. Her touch was all the best things, like warmth after cold, or cool water when you're thirsty. She said, "Only you, Angka, danced it as it should be danced."

And she was gone.

If she went out by the doors I don't know. I think probably she did, so as not to appall the banqueters more than she already had.

When I got up the King was morosely cutting into the baked hedgehog, as if nothing had happened. And a piece of the monkey's orange had gone into the fifth Favorite's ear.

I, too, left, with the minimum of display as befitted my nonexistent rank.

═══

FIRST THING in the morning there was a scene.

When Talu opened the door to her imperious Twenty-sixth-Wife-I-tell-you-I-*am*-important knock, my mother flounced into my bedchamber with her full panoply of two slaves.

"I have never," cawed my mother, "been so humiliated—"

"Oh, you have," I said, "lots of times."

"To make my daughter dance seventeenth and *last*," exclaimed my mother, "and so poorly, I hear the guest left at once."

Something made me say, though I'd resolved all through my wakeful night not to, "She was a goddess and could leave when she liked."

My mother glossed that over. "Get up at once. We must all go to the Main Temple this morning."

"Why?" I asked. I wondered if anyone other than a slave, or myself, would dare admit the truth now it was over.

But, "Lightning struck the obelisk of the Nine Thousandth Ancestor, and your father," said my mother, "is afraid we may have a plague if we don't offer something. I think it will be sheep," she appended fastidiously.

Outside, the sun was burning a big hole in the sky; the only two things without a tarnish of dust. We trundled along the mud roads in our rusty chariot, under a slave-held sunshade. The slave, outside the shade, looked ready to faint, but the people who faint first are always the guard. Three went down as we arrived, flat on their faces. It always surprises me they don't break their noses when they do this. Perhaps they do.

"Hurry, we're late," hissed my mother, as if we mattered.

In the open square before the temple stood my father with the chief priest. Elsewhere were Wives, other priests droning, citizens with time to spare.

My mother and I arrived at our platform, more crowded than the King's and more out of sight.

Above the temple rose a rounded hill, clad with beehive-shaped tombs looking like lots of fat stone people come to stare. I thought of the goddess, and the daughter of the goddess, who was buried under the earth.

The guard carrying the banner fainted and was hastily replaced.

After the prayers the royal party, in which we were just included, went into the temple to watch the sheep being sacrificed, and then something quite weird happened. No sooner was the first sheep lifted to the altar than it gave a fierce bleat, leaped over my father's head, and pelted for the exit, followed by its friends. Everybody scattered, as if they were being charged by lions or wild boar. The sheep sprinted out into the city and disappeared into the maze of alleys behind the temple.

Everyone was left looking more sheepish than the sheep had looked. The escape was considered an ill omen.

"Your father," said my mother, "will be most annoyed." She said this loudly, in case anyone might be listening who would immediately deduce that it was important to the King that the Twenty-sixth Wife foresaw he would be annoyed. I watched her admiringly.

I thought: Suppose I had died and vanished under the earth—what would my mother do? Would she wander all the lands like a beggar, weeping when she saw some girl who, for a fleeting moment, had a look of me? But I knew perfectly well what my mother would and wouldn't do. She'd sob and scream and blame everyone, not excepting me, and soon she would forget me but for the odd, mawkish minute that might be useful in engaging someone's sympathy for her.

There was no sacrifice that day. We went back to the palace.

———

THE STORM was late that evening, and some doomsayers were out in the city claiming we were under a curse and now there would be a drought. Then the skies opened and thunder, rain, and lightning crashed down through the overgrown Sun Garden, hitting the pagoda roof like a gong.

Talu and I sat in the porch, preparing vegetables for our supper, watching the rain.

"Tell me about the goddess," I said.

"I? A mere sl—"

"Stop it, Talu," I snapped, exactly like my mother. "No one will talk about it. It's as if it didn't happen. And before it happened it was as if it wasn't going to. Only you told the truth."

Talu was flattered. Her iron hair quivered. So she recited to me what she knew.

"She's an elder goddess. Yes, she looks young enough, but she's centuries old. Her daughter she had by the god of the thunder, black browed and golden eyed. . . . But then her daughter, tainted with the mortal world where she'd wandered about such a lot, she died. That's how it is with children. You let them go to play in the garden and something bad happens to them. They eat a poison apple, or a snake gets them."

"*Talu.*"

"Well, some say it was a disease that killed her, or a snake's bite, or that a man, or even a god, carried her off. But she went away under the ground. And ever since, the goddess has searched for her over the earth, looking for the spot where she went down." Talu split a root with a nasty, tactless crack. Then she paused, gazing away through the rain and trees. "But you see, she knows she'll find her again, one day, her girl. She'll come up through the black soil like the first flower of spring, like the green corn. So the goddess looks and looks. And now and then she sees a human girl who reminds her, and then the goddess weeps the stars. So they say."

I suddenly saw that Talu's eyes had tears in them. Unlike the flawless goddess, she snuffled and wiped her nose with the back of her sleeve—*not* by any means the procedure with which she had indoctrinated me.

"I had a daughter," said Talu, "who died before she was a year old. Every mother fears that."

I thought of my mother in the room by the colonnade, eating cakes, batting her long-suffering slave with a fly whisk.

I put my arm around Talu for three whole seconds. Then I kicked my sandals across the room so she could scold me and pick them up, and went to tangle my hair for her.

R O B E R T   W E S T A L L

Fifty-fafty

FRIDAY AFTERNOONS, my mother picked me up from school and we went shopping down the town. Out of our leafy suburb, down into the smoky jungle. Wondrous shops were there, full of Dinky Toys and pink ladies' corsets. But the poor were there, too. Beyond the shops, all down to the river, they got poorer and poorer. In the lower depths they Drank and had no drains; emptied their soapy washing-up water and worse straight into the furrows of yellow-clay paths that trickled, in the end, into the black waters of the Tyne, iridescent with the sick beauty of oil and awash with broken fish boxes, where only the inedible blackjack swam, caught by boys who had no boots or shoes, and left lying to rot on the cobbled quays. Where dirty women hung out of windows and shouted incomprehensible things as you passed, and did incomprehensible things with sailors, then cut their throats as they slept and lifted their wallets and dropped their bodies straight into the river through trapdoors in their houses.

I don't remember how old I was. I know I had sadly abandoned hope of dragons. I had checked for wolves under the stairs and found only a sack of musty potatoes and a meter with the faint, exciting whiff of gas. But there were still monsters. The lamplighter walking in front of us was a minor wizard. He put up his long pole to the gas lamps and created darkness. It was broad daylight till the gas lamps flared; instantly, night gathered around them like smoke. My own headmaster was a fabulous monster of sorts. Tiny, bent, wizened, and silver haired, we loved him. But the boys said that he had once been a six-foot sergeant major in the Welsh Guards, broad as a house with a voice like a bull. Till the gas got him, in the Battle of the Somme. And down the town there were much more satisfying monsters like Happy Ralph, who lurked at the bottom of Borough Road and rushed out at you with outstretched arms and incoherent cries, whether to embrace you or strangle you nobody ever lingered to find out. On Sundays, Happy Ralph went from church to church, roaming the aisles and terrifying the vicars in their pulpits and the spinsters in their pews.

A trackless safari into the dusk. But not without waterholes. First my aunt Rose's house, only a little way into the jungle, where people still holystoned their doorsteps and polished their knockers daily. But Aunt Rose was definitely a denizen of the jungle, her living room long and dark as a dungeon, only a pale ghost of daylight trickling in past aspidistra and lace curtain, over the massive overstuffed three-piece crowded like cattle in a byre.

She gave us tea, which we balanced on our knees. She stayed on her feet, solid as a bullock in her flowered pinafore, hair in a tight black bun, and railed against God.

At home, God was the God of green grass and fresh air and Sunday best, the Vicar in spotless black and white, missions to save the Africans from naked sinfulness and roast beef for dinner after. But down where Aunt Rose lived God prowled like a man-eating tiger, driving good men to drink by killing their young wives with TB and slaughtering innocent babes in their cradles. And not one of his evil tricks escaped Aunt Rose's eagle eye.

"How could He do it?" she would thunder. "To a little innocent lamb who had done no wrong?" as she stood against the oaken altar of her sideboard, arrayed with photographs of the dead of whom God had robbed her. I treasured her as I never treasured our Vicar. The Vicar had God on his side, was teacher's pet. My aunt Rose stood and thundered, fearless and alone. She couldn't possibly win against God . . . could she? Still, I could imagine her smashing through the Pearly Gates, blazing out accusations like a Medium Tank.

My mother saw it differently. Pale, prim, and pious, she sat through Aunt Rose's sermons in silence and walked silent down the street afterward. Glancing up slyly I would see a furtive tear trickle down her cheek. Often, afterward, my father would shout at her, demanding to know why she bothered going to Rose's at all? All she would ever say, white as a stone, was "Blood is thicker than water."

Then I would see the dead sailors' blood, thick as Tate and Lyle syrup, red as Heinz tomato sauce, coiling up through the black, oily waters of the Tyne.

===

NEXT STOP, the Co-op on Howdon Road. Sawdust on the floor, full of footprints where the bare floorboards showed through; sawdust that was carried by departing feet across the wet pavements for miles around. You could have tracked your way to the Co-op without ever raising your head, just by following the sawdust prints. There was a fat black-and-white cat, sitting on a sack of loose dog biscuits, licking sawdust off its fur; whole sides of smelly bacon, hanging from floor to ceiling; round blocks of dewy butter and cheese, big as barrels; gleaming brass weights and Jack Sylph.

Jack Sylph was also a magic monster, more magic even than my aunt. I knew from poems that I'd learned that a "sylph" was a slender, naked female. Jack, though undeniably thin, was also undeniably male and clad in a long, brown coat, with a yellow pencil behind his ear. And though his face was young he was as totally bald as a polished egg. Did he polish his head every morning with a duster, after he'd cleaned his teeth? Did he use furniture polish on it? As my aunt used polish on the photo frames of her dead? My mother said he'd been bald ever since he was eighteen, yet he had courted and married and had four children. I thought of his wife, waking up in the dark, and feeling for that warm, bald, polished egg, as I still reached for my teddy bear.

Jack was a wizard, too. He could cut you a piece of cheese any weight you wanted. My mother always asked for odd weights, just for the pleasure of seeing him do it.

"Six and three-quarter ounces, please, Jack." He draws himself up to a great height, his eyes as keen as Don Bradman scoring a six. Down comes the cheese wire. On to the scales . . . exactly right. My father says he should be on the music halls.

And he makes up her order without ever stopping asking about her family. "I'm glad her sciatica's better . . . and a pound of washing soda." His head talks and all the time his clever white hands are reducing whatever bags, tins, drums, or packets she has bought into an exact geometrical cube, wrapped in brown paper, and tied with string, with a double loop at the top for her to put her fingers through to carry it.

Next, to Tawse's the drapers, where my mother used to work before she married. Tawse's is a cliff, twelve foot high, of shelving behind the counter. There are ladders nearly as high as firemen's ladders, up which the assistants run to lift down enormous, overwhelming boxes and rolls of cloth. My mother has a huge dent in her shin where she used to lean into the rung of the ladder when she raised both arms to lift something down. Sometimes, on evenings round the fire, I grow fascinated by it, press on it, ask her if it hurts. She doesn't wince. I ask her if she was scared, up the cliff; she says she got used to it.

My mother, after endless pursing of her mouth and feeling the material between finger and thumb, proving she is no fool and has been in the business to the young chits who are working there now, makes her purchase and hands over her ten-shilling note, for a pair of rayon stockings at one and elevenpence threefarthings.

Now is the big moment. The assistant screws the bill and the note into a round wooden cylinder a bit like a shell. She loads it into a cage. . . . I look at the ceiling. There is a kind of miniature tramway screwed along the ceiling. The assistant pulls a lever and the wooden shell whizzes along the tramway like a rocket with a fearful rattle, just like a tram, and vanishes into a mysterious little wooden house marked CASHIER. After two minutes, the shell comes rocketing back, with the receipted bill and, magically, the correct change in it.

Why does that person hide inside that blank wooden box? Has he no legs, like the man who sings songs for money from a little trolley at the top of Saville Street? Or is he hideously deformed, like the midnight mechanics who empty the earth closets in the cart-rumbling lamplit dark and never show themselves by daylight, because their faces are eaten away by unmentionable mysterious diseases?

Out into the rainy street. My mother takes my arm in hers now. For the unemployed men were squatting in groups at every street corner, passing a smoldering fag-end round between them, smoking it down to the last quarter-inch by impaling it on a pin they take from the lapels of their coats. You could see the heads of a row of pins, gleaming in each of their lapel tops, for they had turned up their collars against the drizzle. They pick up the pins from the ground, like they pick up fag-ends.

It is not that my mother is afraid of anything the men might do or say to her. They dwelt in a world of their own, their heads much nearer the ground, their cracked boots polished till they shone like diamonds, their white mufflers spotless, their caps as sharp-set as the brave soldiers they once were. Wearing their hopeless pride like a wall. No, we did not fear them; but we feared what had happened to them. As if unemployment was infectious, like diphtheria or scarlet fever that could pass through the air from their very breath. My father is employed, at the gasworks. His work muffler is filthy; he never has time to clean his boots. He is busy working.

Last stop, the chemist's. It glows through the dark like a jewel, huge globes with pointed stoppers, two feet high, full of mysterious liquid, red, blue, green, enough to poison the whole town. And inside, more huge jars with unreadable names. SOD BIC. AQUAE FORTIS. CANT MEM. Rows of varnished drawers full of wickedness.

But the most terrifying thing about him is the way he speaks. He speaks posh, posher than anyone I've ever heard. My mother wants some Sal Hepatica. I am always encouraging her to buy Sal Hepatica. Every time we set out for town I ask her whether she has enough. The medicine chest in the bathroom must be full of it; I don't even know what she uses it for. But I long to hear this chemist echo her, with his utterly eerie voice.

"Sal Hair-pair-teeh-caaah." It sounds like a spell; like the names of one of the Pharaohs in school, or of those volcanoes in Mexico.

In the street again, I chant it to the night. "Saaaal Heeeeep-eeeeeh-tiiiii-caaaah. Saaaaal Heeeeep-eeeeeh-tiiic-caaaaah." My mother tells me to stop; it is rude. So I chant "Tuuuutaaaankaaaamu" and "Coootooopaaaxi" instead.

And so to Nana's for tea. Her front door opening at a touch; my mother's timid "Yoo-hoo" echoing through the church-like gloom of the cold front hall. Then the kitchen door opened, the red light, the blast of heat from the kitchen range, the sweet, overpowering smell of baking bread, and Nana, up to her elbows in white flour, wiping her pink, perspiring forehead with the back of her hand and adding more white streaks to what was there already. Behind her, the kitchen range gleams black and silver in the red gloom, and on the mantelpiece all the horsebrasses and ornaments, polished till they, too, gleam silver. Nana polishes things to within an inch of their life.

Half the table oilcloth is covered already with the plump, white, female shapes of finished bread, cooling on wire grids. Inside the gleaming brass fender, great cloth-covered bowls, where domes of white female dough rise inexorably every time you lift the cloth to peep. And yet more white dough, twisting between Nana's strong hands.

"Sit yourselves down," she says, with a gasp of exhausted glee. "Give the bairn a bun, while they're hot."

At home, I might be made to wait. Not here. Here I am a little king. I can have all the buns I can eat. Instantly. Till I am sick, though I never am. That is her way, that is part of her magic.

The smell of the opened bun, the smell of the running, melting butter. The heat of the fire on my face, turning to pricks of perspiration on the back of my neck. The black horsehair sofa prickles against the backs of my knees, under my short trousers. My grandmother is a white bread-witch, solid and strong as her rising dough, and I am safe in her kingdom.

When I was born, my mother had a bad time. She often tells me and I feel dreadful guilt. Afterward, she was too weak to carry me in her arms. But my grandmother carried me about everywhere, till I was three. My father often says, in a quietly glad voice, "Your Nana's a strong woman."

Yet she's as quick to joke as a child. Once, when my grandfather was washing at the kitchen sink, stripped to the waist, after work, she held a handful of snow against his bare back. His mouth flew open with the shock. His false teeth fell out, and Nana still gets helpless with laughter when she remembers.

Sometimes, she still takes in stray men as lodgers. Lost dogs, down on their luck. An ex–army major, full of wondrous stories about pig sticking in India, but often still shell-shocked and shaking with black memories of the trenches. The first Oriental merchant in the town, a carpet seller called Ali Hassan. He is prospering greatly now, but he still calls every year to bring her a Christmas present. He sits at the table in a turban, with two turbaned grown-up sons standing respectfully behind him, waves his jeweled hands and tells her stories and gives her huge drums of Turkish Delight. The real stuff, not Cadbury's rubbish; wooden boxes with Turkish writing on the side, powdered white, which I share while he is still sitting there. He is more exciting than Charlie Chan in the movies.

=====

My mother realizes she has forgotten to buy my father's cigarettes.

"Run along back, hinny. You've just got time, before he comes," says Nana.

I am alone with my magic woman.

She says, "Eeh, where've I put my oven cloth?" I giggle, because I can see it hanging over her shoulder. She follows my eyes and finds it.

"Eeh, Aah'm daft. Aah'd forget me head if it was loose."

I say, "Fifty-fafty, you're a dafty." I wouldn't dare say that to my mother. She would say it was rude. Nana doesn't care. Instead, she says, "Do you know who Fifty-fafty was?"

"No. It's just something we shout to each other at school. I didn't know it was a person."

Her eyes grow thoughtful. "Oh, aye, he was a person, all

right. Poor bugger. But you don't want to hear about him. . . ."

"I do." I know she is only teasing. There is a story coming up. There is a glint of excitement in her eye.

She draws herself together, like Jack Sylph cutting cheese.

"He was a poor boy. Born down by the river. Fishermen. Hadn't two pennies to bless themselves with."

I shiver deliciously; they put two pennies on the eyes of dead people.

"Anyway, Fifty-fafty was bright. He could see there wasn't any money in fishin', so he ran away to sea to make his fortune. Just like Bobby Shaftoe. An' when he went, he took his father's silver ring. The family heirloom, the only thing they had worth tuppence.

"Well, they cursed him an' forgot him. All except his sister—he'd been closest to her. An' they got poorer and poorer. Aah can't tell ye the things they had to do to make ends meet."

I shiver again; I know the things they do, down by the river.

"An' then, one day, years later, this grand rich man comes to the town—wearing a fur coat and so many rings on his fingers it was dazzlin'. He was buyin' drinks for everybody he met. He was the talk of the town. But he had a great beard coverin' his face, an' he wouldn't tell anybody his name. An' that night he wouldn't stay at the inn—he walked down to the river and sought out that family an' asked them if they could put him up for the night. An' they looked at his fur coat an' rings, an' the great bag he carried, an' they said they could. And at supper, and all the time till bedtime, he talks about the places he'd been an' the wonderful things he'd seen, an' of all the ships and land and houses he owned.

"An' just afore bedtime, he catches the sister outside, an' swears her to secrecy an' tells her who he is. It was Fifty-fafty. He showed her the ring an' she believed him, even after all those years. He had come back, like he had promised all those years ago, to make them all rich, so they could live like lords. She begged him to tell everybody straightaway. But he wanted to give them the big surprise he'd worked an' slaved for all those years. An' it was Christmas Eve, an' his big bag was full of presents for them. . . . An' she couldn't do nothing about it—'cos he'd sworn her to secrecy. So she went to bed, upstairs with her mam.

"And in the morning, when she came down, her father and brothers were all laughing and winking at each other, and there was no sign of Fifty-fafty. They said he'd had to leave early, to catch a boat on the tide.

"An' then she knew what had happened. They'd killed him in the night, when he was asleep, an' robbed him in the dark. It was his dead body that had sailed out on the tide, not a ship.

"An' then she burst out weeping and told them about the ring. An' they took out the stuff they'd stolen, an' there was his father's ring they'd slipped off his finger in the dark and never noticed.

"An' they fell to blaming and quarreling, and word got to the magistrate an' they were all hanged. When they could've lived like lords.

"An' that's the story of Fifty-fafty."

She sighed. "If only he'd listened to his sister."

I was silent, and she was silent. Then she finished kneading the last of the dough and set it to rise. And I thought of Fifty-fafty, and all his work and all his hopes, and the way he died, his throat cut in the dark, like a beast, on Christmas Eve. And the way, for hundreds of years, he had haunted the school-yards, with the boys shouting, "Fifty-fafty, you're a dafty." Poor Fifty-fafty, would they never let him rest? Would his daftness live on, to the end of time, in the boot-stamping dead-fly toilets, in the rain-soaked schoolyards?

And then my mother came back, with my father's cigarettes. And then my father came from work, all grinning and greasy and black with his job, with his three-pound paypacket in his pocket. And Nana made the fire up and we had a slap-up tea with bacon and eggs and new bread. And Nana drew her dark red velvet curtains against the rain and the dark. And we were snug, as we always were.

But I listened to the wind and the rain, and thought how thin the glass of the window was, and out there was Fifty-fafty, at the bottom of the sea still, his blood that was thicker than water coiling up through the black depths, like the slime from a rotting cod's head. And Jack Sylph who lost all his hair at eighteen, and the unemployed men squatting on the corners when it was not their fault, and the man-eating God who killed good men's young wives with TB and drove them to drink, and my headmaster who had shrunk in the poison gas of the Somme. . . .

And I cried for them all, quite suddenly.

My father was furious with me, saying I was going on like a wet girl. I had never seen him cry; I don't think he ever did. When I told him about Fifty-fafty, he said Nana had just told me the story of an old play she'd seen years ago at the old Theatre Royal. It wasn't true. But why should the boys call out about Fifty-fafty if he was just some old play?

My mother said, rather proudly, that I had too vivid an imagination, just like her.

But Nana marveled at the softness of my heart.

I was glad for once, that night, to get back up into the green suburb. It was some years still, before I realized that God prowled up there as well.

Dogfaerie

THERE IS some folk what say there bant no such creatures as faeries, but I knows different, see. Them folk is cockle-headed, as any totter, diddycoy, pikey, and tinker would tell. Here's a tale as is proof of such.

More'n a hundred years since, a traveling man took himself from a life on the seaways to settle in the county of Rutland, far north of here. This man built himself a big house on a hill, making use of the woodland trees what covered his estate. While the house were being built, the seed of a dogfaerie blowed in from the woods and growed down below the floorboards. Soon after, afore this wildrose faerie were able to let go its roots, the forest had been cut back to a thicket, situated too far from the dwelling for the dogfaerie to reach. There were no escape for the little creature and it were trapped, tight and hard. Leastways, there were *one* way it could get out, but that were a drastic method, which the dogfaerie were not up to using at that time.

In the beginning, it were happy, see. The master married and filled the house with children, fizzy as lemonade, and the dogfaerie's eating habits were such it gobbled their feelings, the way we would a hunk o' cheese and bread. Them were days when the house smelled of fresh-cut timber and the oak and elm were still in it. The dogfaerie were much like a shrunk child itself, with gold tracers in its eyes, a-flashin' like polished brass on a harness.

Come winter the dogfaerie would curl up in the fire ashes, after all had gone to bed, to keep out the cold. Summertime, though, would find it crawling a-tween the kindling sticks, which was not likely to be touched at that point in the seasons. Fireplaces, with their stacked logs and smell of the forest, is true heart-o'-home for dogfaeries, and where they spend much of their forevers.

O' course, when folk was about the house, it spent much of its forever in hiding. It had the magic of shape changers, so long as there were a copying image in sight, near human form. Like a statue or painting and such. It would stand close to, its eyes burning like candle flames in a draft, and make itself into a copy of that painting afore burying itself deep in the brushstrokes. From that hidey-hole it would set to studying the folk coming and going, as snug and safe as wood worms in a beam. Folks would look on the eyes of such pictures and shiver awhile from their toes without knowing the wherefores.

On such close-to lookings from human folks, the dogfaerie took to having feelings what bant known to you or me. It were both caught and thrown by such close proximities, since it liked the nearness of human folk but hated the stink of a real living soul. One Edward Ruttersdown, owner of this house at the century's change, would lean with his back up at the fireplace, warming his trouser seat, never knowing what gases wafted from his soul and all but choked the poor dogfaerie's delicate senses.

Later on, of course, the house were full of photos, pictures of the family, old folks and babes, and the dogfaerie would flit from one to other, changing places as quick as a weasel swapping holes.

Listen in, though. There were one image what frit that dogfaerie more than Oberon himself: its very own likeness. When it stood to, afore a mirror and looking on its own form, it knew it were standing on the cliff edge of nowheres—of nowheres in nothingworld. A dogfaerie is eternal, never dying, but take away itself and there is nothing to hold it inside. If the dogfaerie went into its own image, inside the mirror, it would vanish away, for a looking-glass picture is only as lasting as the folk what stands afore it, be they human or faerie.

One night in May-time, when the cherry blossoms were covering the windowpanes with pollen dust in the darkness, Edward Ruttersdown spoke a few words to his good wife. "Darlin'," he says, soft as you like, "the two of we must go from this here house and find another home. Business in London calls us to it, and we must move to the big city."

"Oh," she says in a voice what is tight with feeling, "and why might that be?"

"The business," he tells her, "has got to have me near it, now it's growed so big. There is a grand lady by the name of Wuthers, wishing to buy this old house with good cash. I will buy you a fine home in the town. I know you will like it as well as this one."

"Well," she says, looking around wistful like, "I don't know as I'll like no place as well as this, but if it's got to be I won't cause no argument. But let me tell you this, Teddy Ruttersdown, I shall miss our home, despite its funny ways."

The dogfaerie were naturally very saddened to hear these words from the human folk of the household. It wanted to make them stay, but such power were not in its tiny hands. It could do many things, play many tricks with light and shadow, and send whispering voices from the woodwork of empty rooms. It could drive out spiders, silver the flies, and gild the cockroaches. It could copy the bats and birds in the attic, their sounds, and leave peculiar scents in the corners of the hall. But it could not make the humans stay and be happy with their lot.

"And another thing," says Alice Ruttersdown, as she looks up from her embroidering to the photo of her mother above the fireplace, "have you told this Wuthers lady that the house is haunted with a ghost? No, I can see it in your face you haven't."

"Well," says her Teddy, shifting his bottom as the hot coals send up steam from his shiny pants, "it would only give her the frits, and she's an old lady. The ghost won't harm her none and she's a very shortsighted woman, deaf as a post with it."

"Come away from that fire before it scorches," says Alice. And Teddy does as he's told in such small matters as this, knowing he has got the big one under his wing.

So the house fell into the wrinkled hands of its last mistress. Widow Wuthers were an ancient piece of flesh, dry as a husk of corn let lie in the sun. Her body had not the spark of the child still residing: all her feelings was stale and untasty, leaving a bitter flavor on the dogfaerie's tongue. The dogfaerie came to loathe her bad, since she would chase off young people what come to the garden. Once it even showed itself, but she spit at it and raised up her stout hickory stick as if to strike. She were concerned by nothing in this life, for death were waiting not far off, crouched and ready to jump on her shoulders, and this squatter in her home worried her no more than ghosts or faeries.

The Wuthers woman did nothing to make repairs on the house, and slowly the place fell into ruins from where it would not rise again. When the unwelcome squatter finally leaped and bore her creaky frame to the floor under its weight, the garden had growed tall with weeds what choked the air and fluffed up the drainpipes with white seed balls, the windowsills of the house had rotted and new tenants moved into the cupboards on insecty legs. Widow Wuthers were taken away to her last narrow home, but no new folk came to fill the old place and stock its larder with tears or laughter.

Silence unpacked its bag and settled in.

The dogfaerie had a melancholy hunger. It missed, most of all, the scampering feet and voices of the children. Now it had only the wind in the chimney. Mice scuttled to and fro behind wainscots and nameless birds stamped across the roof, hollering at their own kind. On occasion, slates did death slides down the roof, to crash on the paths underneath. Moss crept in through chinks in the brickwork, and toadstools growed on the inside ledges.

In the shafts of light what sparkled with dust, the dogfaerie sat and moped, its spirit growing lean. All around, the house shed its finery and the damp of the cellars moved up to the bedrooms.

The dogfaerie hated it. And it were not too long afore this hatred sizzled and spat like it were frying in grease, and this meal of emotions it were cooking were intended to be served to human folk, once they came into reach again. Humans had built the house, had trapped the faerie inside one of their dwellings, and lastly, had left it there to pine and starve. On days when Jack Frost twinkled in the grasses outside the windows and copied the patterns of ferns on the panes themselves, the dogfaerie would go to the great oval mirror standing proud in the hall and think about what shouldn't be thought. It would take to staring at itself, its shape, born of dog rose and bryony during a stalking moon, and try to summon up its strength to enter nothingness, never getting there.

One day in spring it sat licking the cobwebs clean of housefly terror, when it seen two figures come into the garden. One were a tall man with black hair and a face bearing the marks of eighty winters. The other were a small boy with seven summers in his eyes. This pair had come in the grounds through a gap in the old redbrick wall where ivy had tore out the mortar. They had fishing rods in their hands and they talked in high voices of finding the large pool half hidden by thistles.

"This is a good place," says the boy. "An't nobody been here for years, have they, Grandpa? You can see that from the thistles. Nobody likes thistles in their garden, do they, Grandpa, eh?" And he laughs.

Fifty years since, the dogfaerie would have loved to hear that laugh, but now it rose fury in it. There were happiness outside, in the wilds of outdoors. It wanted to get to the little boy and poke his eyes out with a twig.

"Can't argue that, little man," says the child's companion. "Shouldn't think nobody's been here since the old woman died, when I were a boy. Long climb up that hill. And not much when you get here, except a few old crab apples. Place is filled with wilderness."

"But it's got this here pond," says the boy.

"Yep, the pond looks good. Shouldn't wonder there's a fish or two, 'neath that scumweed. Get a line out, boy—let's see what's what."

So the pair settled in to fish and chatter the sunshine away, while the dogfaerie fumed in the dust and damp of the house.

Later that night, when a rash of stars lighted up the garden, the dogfaerie set to scheming. There were one way it could leave the house, but it meant giving up its faerie form forever. It could, should it wish, take over and possess a child. In the same way it entered images, it could change its form to resemble the little boy and then take over his body. But to do this terrible thing, it had to get the child inside the house.

It gathered from all the nooks and crannies of the house the cast-off feathers of birds. It took some moss from one of the sills in the larder, and some clay what had seeped through cracks in the cellar walls. With these it wove a strange bird, which were sure to catch the eye of the little boy. The tail feathers was all of different lengths and the wings like the flaps of a child's kite. The beak were the tip of a dead rat's tail and the eyes come from two black beetles. Dried spiders made up the claws, and its breast were fashioned of dandelion down, blown in fresh from the garden.

The dogfaerie put this decoy just inside the doorway of the house, where the great door hanged loose on its hinges, and waited for the return of the small boy.

The couple did not come for many days, and though dog-faeries is eternal, time passes by as slowly for them as any human folk when nothing but expectancies float in the still air around their heads. Its tiny heart were pattering fast as it doodled with a splinter in the dust, waiting, waiting.

Just when hope were all but dry mold in its breast, it heard the sound of voices on the breeze. Into the sunlighted garden come the boy and his grandfather. They stared at the house for a handful of moments, and then the boy tugged at the man's sleeve and pointed at the pond.

They sat down by the water, amid cow parsley, and began to fish. Once or twice the child looked toward the house, but he showed no desire to wander near. The afternoon drifted away and the dogfaerie took to agitation. All it knowed of children told it that the boy would come, that boys like this was curious creatures by nature, following in the footsteps of cats.

Then comes that magical time, just near to sunset, when windows catch such violence as twilights want to offer, show-ing red and fierce reflections in their panes. The human folks showed no signs of leaving. Indeed, the man were intent on his line, fixing the fish with his determined stare.

The young boy, however, were watching the clouds of midges coming in and the low-flying martins dipping in to meet them.

"Hey," cries the boy, jumping up on his feet. "Look, Grandpa, the house is on fire!"

The man looks up, briefly, but says no, it's only the sunset snared by the window glass.

"I'm going to look," cries the child, and begins running to meet the house, while the man shouts to be careful, not to go inside as the boards is all rotten.

The dogfaerie's heart, small as that of a shrew, twitters inside it. The boy were coming. He were running to the house.

The boy stands at the bottom of the wooden porch steps, which lay at all angles and even have weeds poking sly heads through steps and rise.

Up! Climb up!

One foot on the bottom step, testing for strength.

Yes! Yes! Come. See the pretty bird.

Small, light feet, finding their way to the top, to stand on the porch.

A hand on the crumbling doorjamb, skin as soft, pink and delicate as the vanes of a mushroom.

See. See. Look at the pretty bird.

The child's eyes open wide and blue as autumn skies.

"Hey! There's somethin' here. There's a funny bird. . . ."

"Be careful," calls the man.

"It bant moving. Just sittin' still."

"Mind the boards," says the man.

One foot—

      two feet—

           inside.

The dogfaerie flashed bright as new gold, inside, quick as quick. Inside, deep inside the boy. The boy were caught, the boy were . . . something were wrong. The dogfaerie felt the boy's feelings, thought the boy's thoughts, and knowed that there had been no surprise. The child were in a thrall of triumphant feeling, knowing what he already knowed would happen.

"*Got you!*" yells this boy, dashing from the house and

down the wooden steps toward the man what stands, broad in his smile, by the pond.

"Grandpa, Grandpa, I got him."

There is slaps of delight.

"I just knowed you would. From the first day we see the house, I said there were one inside, didn't I, boy? It looked so right. No ghost, said I—that's one of *them* in there."

The boy looks up into the man's face.

"Will I live forever, too, Grandpa? Now I've got him? Like you, Grandpa?"

The black-haired man with the gold-flecked eyes ruffles the boy's hair.

"Sure you will, son. And anybody says to you they don't believe in faeries, why you can tell 'em different, see. You can tell 'em the truthfulness of the thing."

And that's what I done, here in this book.

L I S A   T U T T L E

The Walled Garden

WHEN I was five years old I saw the future. My future. After that, I was unable just to wait and let it happen. I had to go looking for it.

My sister Jean is three years older than me. As children we shared a room and had the same bedtime. I can remember her complaints about being treated like a baby—like me— and put to bed while it was still light. A docile child myself, I would sleep whenever I was told, but Jean, grumbling and protesting, kept me awake as long as she could, for company. She talked to me, and she told me stories. She loved making up stories; she loved things that had not happened. She pulled me along to explore the land of What-if: What if we moved to a different house, or what if we came home from school one day and there was no one here? What if all the grown-ups disappeared? What if people came from another planet and took us away in their flying saucer? When I was

45

very young, it's true, she confused me with her questions and her stories, so that sometimes I lost track of what was real and what only imagined. She made me want a life that didn't exist; she made me cry for the loss of things I'd never known.

One summer night when I was five and Jean was eight, as I remember, she was particularly restless. Outside, it was still as light as day, a fact the thin curtains drawn across the windows couldn't disguise. I lay there in my little bed, twin to hers, patiently waiting for Jean to begin one of her stories, when all at once my sister sat bolt upright.

"It's not fair," she said. "It's not time for bed; it's *not*. Everybody else is still out. I'll bet you the Kellermans are still playing Fox-and-Hounds. Let's go out."

"We're in our pajamas," I said.

"So? In China people wear their pajamas all the time; that's the only kind of clothes they have. Anyway, you've been out in your pajamas before."

"They won't let us."

"They won't *know*," she said. "We're going to escape." She suddenly leaped up and onto my bed. I squealed, pulling in my legs to protect my stomach, but Jean had no intention of tickling me. She'd only come onto my bed to open the window. I watched, thrilled and baffled. Warm air and the scent of freshly cut grass slipped into the room.

"What are you going to *do*?"

"I told you. Escape. I'm going exploring. Do you want to come, or are you going to stay here like a baby and sleep?"

Jean and I lived with our parents in a three-bedroom, one-story house in Beverly Oaks, a suburban subdivision of Houston. It was a desirable, middle-class neighborhood, which had been built soon after the war. The houses—all single-family dwellings!—had attached two-car garages and well-kept lawns and gardens. I had lived there all my life, apart from three days in a downtown hospital when I was born. I knew nothing else. But Jean had spent her first two and a half years in a mysterious place called "the country" on the farm where our grandmother had lived. Grandmother had died, and the farm had been sold, before I was born. I envied Jean that other life I could never know, and I believed she explored the tame suburban streets around us in search of some secret way back to the country. I thought she might find it, too, and I wanted to be with her when she did.

Perched on the windowsill, Jean looked at me, still snug in my bed. She said, "Maybe you'd better not come. It could be dangerous. If somebody saw us—if you weren't careful enough—if you didn't run fast enough—"

I sat up. "I will!"

She shook her head.

"Oh, please!" I said. My sleepiness, my fears, my doubts were forgotten; all in the world I wanted was to follow my big sister. Whatever she wanted, I wanted, too.

"You'll have to do *exactly* what I say."

"Yes, yes!"

"All right, then. Come on. And keep *quiet.*"

Out the window and onto the grass, cool on my bare feet. Jean gripped my shoulder and her voice buzzed in my ear: "Through the Mishners'. If they see us, act normal. Don't rush, but don't stop. Just wave at them and keep on walking."

The Mishners didn't have a fence, so walking through their backyard was the quickest way to get to the alley: It was a shortcut we often took, but with the risk of being captured, for they were an elderly couple always on the lookout for someone, anyone, to interrupt their boredom.

But that evening, fortunately, they were not in sight, and we passed through in safety.

I watched Jean admiringly as I struggled to keep up with her. She was the great explorer, alert to everything, sniffing the air and looking around at familiar fences, gardens, and backs of houses we passed.

When we emerged from the alley onto Warburton Drive, Jean turned left without hesitation. This way would lead us to the bigger houses, the more expensive part of the subdivision. There were a couple of houses over there with swimming pools, and one was known as "the house with the bomb shelter." Jean had told me stories, too, and I remembered one about a fabulous playhouse, full of wonderful toys, built by a wealthy couple for grandchildren who visited them only once a year. If we could find it, we could play there undisturbed.

I grabbed Jean's arm. "Are we going to look for the playhouse?"

"What playhouse? What are you talking about? Don't you know where we are?"

Her tone of voice informed me that we were in the middle of an adventure. I shook my head meekly. "I forgot."

"We're in China. We've just crossed the Gobi Desert. Everyone else on the expedition died—we're the only survivors. Now we're looking for the Forbidden City. No Westerners have ever been allowed to enter it and live, so we shall be the first—unless they catch us—"

At that moment, rounding a bend in the road, three boys on bicycles came into view.

"The Royal Guards!" said Jean. "If they see us, we're dead! We have to split up—you go that way—meet me at the river later if you manage to lose them!"

She was off. I felt panic at being left alone and would have disobeyed her orders and followed, but she could run so much faster than me that she was already out of sight. Meanwhile, the enemy was gaining on me. I turned and ran toward the nearest house, ducking behind a bush for shelter. My heart thudded painfully as I watched the boys cycle past—for a moment I had forgotten that they were only children and believed they would kill me, as Jean had said. When they had gone, I emerged. Now what?

Meet me at the river, she had said, but where was the

river? Like the rest of the territory, rivers were defined according to a map that only Jean could read. A river might be a swift rush of water in the gutter (but the day was dry), or a dip in a lawn, or even a street we would have to pretend to swim across. I decided to start walking in the direction I had seen Jean run and hope that she would come back and find me.

I traveled as Jean would have wanted, as if she were watching me, moving cautiously to avoid being seen, ducking behind bushes and cars, favoring alleys over streets. Gradually I left the familiar landscape behind. The houses were bigger here, the trees shading them were older and larger than those on my street. Golden lights shone from windows. The air was blue with the deepening dusk, and I began to feel afraid. I kept walking, because I didn't know what else to do, but I wondered if every step was taking me farther from Jean and safety and home.

Then I came to a high, brick wall. This was unusual. In my neighborhood there were plenty of wooden and chain-link fences, but I had never seen such a high, brick wall. Jean would have wanted to know what was hidden behind it; she would have climbed over it, I thought.

My heart beat harder. Was Jean nearby? Had she been here before me? Was she already on the other side?

I called her name, but the redbrick surface before me seemed to swallow the sound of my voice, and I knew she wouldn't hear. I flung myself at the wall then, fingers scrabbling at the rough surface. But there was nothing to hold, and so I kept falling back. I jumped straight up, but that was worse than useless. The wall was much too high. I didn't think even my father could have seen over the top of it. And yet, somehow, I had become convinced that Jean was on the other side of the wall. I probably had to believe that because the idea that I might be lost in a strange place at night without my sister was far too frightening.

"Jean," I said, whispering, since I knew shouting wouldn't be any better, and I began to walk beside the wall, trailing my fingers along the rough surface. At the end of the alley the wall curved away and I followed it across the grass, right up to the side of an imposing, two-story, redbrick house. I ran past the front of the house to the other side, and there was the wall again.

And there, in the wall, a door.

The door was very small, made of wood, painted a glossy black. It was an absurdly small door, but at the time the unlikeliness of it did not strike me. The door was smaller even than I was: almost doll-sized rather than child-sized. I crouched down and—there was no handle—pushed it open. It swung slowly inward.

All I could see at first was green grass, the trunks of a few trees, and a flowering bush. I moved forward, on hands and knees, determined to see more. I was a small child, but the doorway was very narrow, and it seemed for a moment that I might stick halfway. But, stubbornly determined, I put my head down and pushed, scraping my shoulders and wriggling my hips, determined and indifferent to discomfort.

And then I was through. I was in the garden, and I had done it all by myself! Wouldn't Jean be proud of me when she knew!

I had to find her. She must be here. Maybe she had found a playhouse or some other wonderful treasure that the high wall had been built to conceal. I ran across the velvety lawn, between spreading oaks and glossy-leaved magnolias, aware of the big house which dominated the garden, although I did not look at it directly. I felt giddy with excitement. I felt as if I was in the middle of a game of hide-and-seek, but I couldn't remember if I were hider or seeker. Years later, trying to remember details, I couldn't recall anything specific that I might not have seen in a dozen other gardens. Just grass and trees and leaves and flowers, greens and darker greens glowing slightly in the twilight. And yet the air, warm on my bare skin, was charged with significance. The lengthening shadows promised mysteries within. The evening held its breath: Something was about to happen.

She saw me first. She saw a child with tangled brown hair and dirty feet, wearing pink pajamas and running in wide circles on the velvety lawn, through the gathering dusk.

The child felt her unexpected presence and froze, like a wild animal, and turned her head, and stared.

There were two of them, a man and a woman. They were standing very close to each other, but not touching. Not yet. He was looking at her. She was looking at me.

We stared at each other as if we knew each other, and yet as if we had never seen each other before. There was something about her that was like my mother—like my mother disguised as someone else. I knew her and yet I didn't. I waited for her to say my name and tell me who she was.

But instead of moving toward me, she half turned to look at the man beside her, and she reached for his hand. Then they were gazing into each other's eyes, a unit which excluded me, and I was suddenly terrified.

———

I SUPPOSE I ran away then. I don't remember what happened next, or how I got home. I must have told Jean about my adventure because we spent the rest of that summer searching in vain for a high brick wall and the garden behind it. We never found it. Jean lost patience, or belief. Her interests led her in other directions. But even though I stopped talking about it, I never forgot. I was sure I would find the walled garden again someday.

I was thirteen, I think, when Jean—who was in high school by then, and dating boys—bought a hair-coloring kit and streaked my hair blonde. I can't remember exactly why: whether I had wheedled, or she had decided it was time her little sister emerged from the cocoon of childhood into a brightly colored adolescence. At any rate, it brought us together. We were happily intimate, perched on stools in the tiny, warm, brightly lit room, inhaling the acrid fumes from my hair while Jean worked with her pencils and brushes and pots and sticks of makeup to redefine my face. We weren't using the mirror that covered the whole wall behind the sink; instead, we gazed solemnly and intently into each other's faces. Every now and then Jean would draw back to look at the effects of her work, and my heart would lift when she nodded with satisfaction. I imagined that she was going to make me over in her own image. At last, I was going to be like Jean—I would be grown-up!

When she was done, Jean took hold of my shoulders and turned me toward the mirror.

"There," she said. "The girl becomes a woman. What do you think?"

The face in the mirror did look like a woman's, and I knew I'd seen that woman before. I stared at eyes larger and more blue, higher cheekbones, a narrower nose, a complexion without freckles, and saw a familiar stranger. I remembered the woman in the garden, and suddenly, finally, I understood. I *knew*. That woman, of course, was me.

Was the garden real? That wasn't the question. The garden *would be* real. I had been privileged to see it, to glimpse my own future, to see myself standing with the man I would love.

I was, of course, very interested in love at that age. I longed for it, for that knowledge that would make me adult. I imagined true love striking once and lasting forever, leading to marriage and eternal bliss. The boys I knew were impossible; as for the men I did desire—actors and pop stars—impossible to imagine them wanting me. All I could do was hope that when I grew up it would be different. And now I *knew* it would be. I had seen the man I was going to love; the man who would love me. It was going to happen. I only had to wait.

The memory of the man in the garden, and the hope he represented, kept me going through the next few, dreadful years. The agonies of high school and dating—or not dating. The miseries of being unchosen. I wasn't popular like my big sister. I wasn't clever, or talented at anything in particular, and although boys did occasionally ask me out, I never had anyone in love with me; I never had a particular, devoted boyfriend the way Jean, so effortlessly, always did.

But I would have my man in the garden, someday. I was alone now, but it wouldn't always be so. I had seen the future. That made me special. That kept me going.

———

I MET Paul in my first year of college. He was a boy in one of my classes, whom I noticed from the first day. Something about him attracted me, and when I made an excuse to talk to him afterward, about the lecture, he seemed nice: serious and a little shy. Then one day, perhaps two weeks into the semester, I was walking across the quad on my way to the library when I quite unexpectedly caught sight of him. He was standing on the grass talking to someone I didn't know. I saw Paul for the first time at a distance, in three-quarters profile. And the way he looked—tall and fair—and the way he stood, bending his neck, stooping slightly to look at the girl beside him, went straight to my heart; a stab of recognition indistinguishable from desire. I knew him. I had always known him. I wanted him.

We were soon dating, and after a few weeks we became lovers. When we spent our first night together I told Paul that he was the man in the garden. He was enchanted. I suppose it made him feel special, maybe for the first time. And he believed me. I became his fantasy as he was mine, and he fell utterly in love with me.

It was first love for both of us, and I don't think that either of us doubted for an instant of those first two months that our love would last forever. Even so, the prospect of Christmas break was devastating. We were still too young—and poor—to consider there might be alternatives to spending the vacation apart, with our parents, at opposite ends of the country. But after seeing each other every day and spending every night together, the prospect of a whole month apart was bleak and rather frightening. I could hardly remember what I had done, what I had thought about before I met Paul. I told him I would write to him every day. He promised to phone as often as he could.

Although I expected to miss Paul unbearably, I couldn't help being excited about going home again. I had missed my parents, and Jean, and I wanted to trade experiences with my old school friends. Above all, I longed to talk to Jean about Paul. I wondered what she would say. At last I had a boyfriend, the way she had for so many years. It made me feel that I had done the impossible and caught up to her: We were equals at last. But I needed her acknowledgment before I could entirely believe it.

Jean's boyfriend for the past two years had been a law student named Bill, and because Jean was now in her last year of college I more than half expected her to announce their engagement that Christmas. Instead, when I asked about Bill, she told me she was no longer seeing him. She was brisk: It was over, he was forgotten. She didn't want my pity, which was a relief. She was my grown-up big sister, who knew so much more than I did, and if she had wanted my comfort I wouldn't have known how to give it. Or maybe that's an excuse for selfishness. I was too full of my new discovery to spare a thought for anything else. I didn't want to talk about Jean's life; I wanted to tell her about Paul.

She was interested and seemed happy for me. She was such a sympathetic, understanding listener that I told her more than I had intended. I told her why I *knew* this was true love, once and forever. I explained how I had recognized Paul as the man I was meant to be with.

At first, she didn't remember our long-ago search for the walled garden, but I persisted with details until I saw it connect, saw the flare of memory in her eyes.

She said: "But that wasn't real—not a real wall, not a real garden—"

I shook my head. "Not real in the usual sense. It wasn't just another house in the neighborhood—it wasn't something we could find and see and visit—not then. But it was—or will be—a real place. What I saw was in the future; somehow or other I traveled in time and glimpsed my own future when I was a kid. Maybe it was a dream, but it was real."

Jean had a very odd look on her face. I didn't know what it meant, but it made me uneasy. And she kept shaking her head. "It wasn't a dream. And it certainly wasn't real."

"What do you mean? I'm not making this up."

"No, I know you're not."

"Then what are you saying? That it's impossible? That things like that can't happen? Well, they can—they do. I *know*: It happened to me. I don't know how, or why, or what it means, but it happened. I remember it; I've remembered it all my life. And now that I've met Paul, it all makes sense."

"God, I don't believe this," said Jean. Her mouth was twitching, and her eyes were shiny. I felt furious with her for treating my precious secret so lightly.

"You don't have to believe me," I said coldly. "I know what happened; I don't need you to—"

"Oh, you're so wrong!"

"What do you know about it? You always think you know so much. Just because you're always reading those old books, just because you're older than me—well, there's some things you *don't* know. This isn't anything to do with you. It happened to me. It's *mine*."

I'd been silly to think we were equals, to think she would ever accept me as her equal. We were squabbling again. I was reduced to shouting and stubbornness, while she had that horribly distant, superior look on her face that meant she was about to demolish me with facts.

"You're wrong there," she said. "It didn't happen to you, and it's not yours. It's mine. It's a story that I made up and told you one night when I couldn't sleep. I was always doing that—you remember—always making up stories. And I found that the best way to keep you awake and listening was if I made up stories about *you*. So I told you that one day when you were out exploring you found a high wall with a little tiny door in it, just big enough for you to squeeze inside. And behind that wall was a garden, and in the garden there were a woman and a man. And the woman looked strangely familiar to you, although you didn't know why. Later, when you tried to find the walled garden again, you couldn't, so eventually you thought you must have imagined it and forgot all about it. Or nearly. Because one day, when you were grown-up and married and living in a house of your own, you went out to walk in your garden, and you saw a little girl staring at you—and it was yourself."

I wished I could wake up. "Why are you *doing* this?"

"I'm not doing anything. I'm telling you the truth."

"You're not. It's not. I don't believe you."

"Why should I lie?"

"I don't believe you could make up a story as good as that. Not when you were eight—not even now."

She laughed. "Oooh, a critic! Well, you're probably right. It probably was too sophisticated for me, then. I probably stole the idea from a comic book or something I saw on television. Most of the stories I told you I got from somewhere else and just changed the names."

I didn't want to believe her. But her certainty was compelling. And why should she lie?

"Why do I remember it, then?" I asked. "I don't remember it like a story—I remember it happening to me."

"Maybe you dreamed about it afterward. After all, you must have been half asleep when I was telling it to you . . . a highly suggestible state."

Later, I thought of reasons why Jean might have lied. Jealousy, the unacknowledged desire to spoil things for me because she couldn't bear to see her little sister happy in love when she herself was so unhappy . . . Or maybe she thought she was telling the truth. Maybe, when I was small, I had told her about the garden and because Jean was the storyteller, not me, she remembered it in retrospect as one of her own stories. Maybe she just couldn't cope with something that contradicted her rational view of the world and had to force it into fiction.

Whatever her reasons, conscious or unconscious, she certainly spoiled any future I might have had with Paul. I didn't want to believe Jean, but old habits were too strong. She was my big sister; she knew best. How could I have believed in something as farfetched as time travel or seeing the future? I felt embarrassed; it was as bad as if I'd gone on into adulthood believing in Santa Claus. And because I had told him, as well as because I had based my love on this myth, I felt ashamed to go back to Paul. I treated him very badly. I dropped him flat, treated him like a stranger when I got back to college, and never explained why, never gave him a second chance.

The man in the garden, though, was not so easily dropped. Faith doesn't have much to do with facts or logic; it's more to do with need, and I obviously needed my memory of the garden. Gradually, despite my attempts to disown it, my faith in the garden returned. I didn't think about it much; I told myself that I'd stopped believing, or I told myself that it didn't matter—but eventually it came back; it was there again, beneath the things I did and thought and felt, just as it always had been.

As the years went by I had other boyfriends, and since they didn't all resemble one another, I don't know how much any of them resembled the man in the garden, if at all. I had seen that man—*if* I had seen him—for no more than a few seconds when I was five years old, and never again since. The only thing I knew for sure was that he had been taller than me. And since I am rather small, the fact that all my boyfriends were taller than me might have been no more than coincidence.

When I was twenty-five, and she was twenty-eight, my sister got married. Her husband's name was Howard Olds, he was eight years older than she was, and he was rich. That was the most impressive thing about him. He was also a lawyer, and he dabbled in local politics, not very successfully. I thought he was boring and conceited, not particularly physically attractive, and—most surprisingly for Jean, who had always admired intellect above all—not even very bright. I wondered if Jean could have stooped so low as to marry a man for his money. I didn't know the grown-up Jean very well. Although we had both moved back to Houston after college, we seldom saw each other except at unavoidable family gatherings. This changed after Jean married Howard. Everything changed after my first visit to their house.

It was a large house in River Bend, a prestigious address in an exclusive neighborhood. It had been built twenty or thirty years ago, a two-story, Georgian-style, brick house set on half an acre of land, well shaded with oaks, pines, pecans, and magnolias. And at the back there was a walled garden.

I'll always remember the first time I saw it. Or perhaps I should say, the second time.

Because, of course, it was the same garden. I knew that, I think, even before I saw it. Jean had invited me for dinner. She was still busy in the kitchen when I arrived, so it was

Howard who took me outside to show me around. Inside the walled garden it was very beautiful and peaceful. I could hear birds, distantly, and the wind in the pines. The air was blueing toward night. I looked around and made polite, admiring noises at whatever Howard pointed out, but I wasn't paying attention to him and hardly heard a word he said. I was far too tense, vibrating inside and out, my nerves and senses all unnaturally sharpened and focused on this moment to which, it seemed, my whole life had been leading. Only one thing mattered. What I was looking for—and praying not to see—was a little girl in pink pajamas.

She didn't come. Yet I couldn't relax. I kept waiting. And when Howard led me back indoors, I don't know if I was more relieved or disappointed. What a joke, if the little girl I had been had seen me with my sister's husband! What a bitter joke, when I had believed I was seeing true love, if I had built my whole life around a misunderstanding.

I must have been a terrible guest that night. I felt such a sense of loss and such undirected bitterness that I couldn't stop brooding. And halfway through the dinner I could not taste I was suddenly struck by a new fear: Did Jean know? Might she guess? Had she recognized the garden? Would she say something? I waited in torment.

But, of course, she didn't know. She had probably entirely forgotten the garden fantasy. Years had passed since that last, bitter conversation about it. It was my experience, not hers. It had never been hers. Of course she didn't remember. At least, I hoped she didn't. I couldn't be sure, because I couldn't ask her without reminding her—and I didn't want that. If it was forgotten, please let it stay forgotten. At any rate, she didn't say anything that night or on future nights.

For there were future nights, despite such a nearly disastrous beginning. I made sure of that. I made friends with Jean and was often invited to dinner. Jean liked giving dinner parties and I became a regular guest. Sometimes I brought a boyfriend, and sometimes she would invite a man for me to meet. I encouraged that, although I never admitted how important it was to me. After the initial shock, I had my faith back again, more strongly than before. I had found the garden I had been looking for. Now, all I had to do was to wait for the right moment to come around again.

I had made a few wrong assumptions, I could see that now. I had imagined that the garden must be mine, or my lover's— but why should that be? It was just a place, after all; a place where anything might happen; a place where something special *would* happen when two times of my life overlapped. I might not meet him there for the first time, but in that garden I would recognize the man who had been meant for me.

Three years passed, and I was not unhappy. Jean and I became friends and shared many things—although I never risked telling her about the garden. She was already playing her part. I began to like Howard better, seeing how happy he made my sister. He wasn't as bad as I had thought, or maybe life with Jean had improved him. And he liked me and flirted with me in a way I enjoyed. I flirted back, meaning nothing by it.

And then, finally, my time in the garden came around again. It was a dinner-party night: Jean and Howard, a couple of neighbors, a junior partner from Howard's firm and his wife, me and Jonathan. Jonathan was a man I had recently met and been out with twice. We hadn't so much as kissed yet—maybe we never would. By that time I had developed quite a strong superstition about the garden and liked to bring men there who were still basically unknown to me, before anything had happened. Howard teased me about all my boyfriends; Jean defended my right to be choosy, praised my good sense in not settling for anything less than exactly what I wanted. I had a few affairs, but I couldn't really, entirely believe in a relationship which blossomed outside the walled garden; I never expected them to last very long or affect me very deeply, and they didn't.

Jonathan was supposed to go into the garden with me. That was my plan. We were walking through the house toward the back when he was sidetracked by one of the other guests who shared some mutual interest. I kept going—the other man was smoking a cigar and I wanted to get away from the smell—trusting Jonathan to follow. But when, in the garden a minute later, I heard someone come out of the house and walk toward me, I didn't need to look around to know that it was Howard.

And then—just then!—I saw myself, the five-year-old in pink pajamas, running across the lawn and then freezing, staring at me, eyes wide and wild as a fawn's.

I felt a moment of disbelief, and then overwhelming despair. Why now? Why did it have to be Howard?

I turned my head to look at him. I was still hoping, I think, that I was wrong, and that it wasn't Howard beside me.

It was Howard, of course, and my glance caught him off guard. I saw how he looked at me, and—I couldn't help myself—I reached for his hand. And as our eyes met, I knew that I could have just what I'd always wanted.

But was this really what I'd always wanted?

Nothing was said. If there had been time, we might have stepped behind the sheltering magnolia and fallen into each other's arms. But we heard the smooth, gliding sound of the patio door and moved apart. I think the motion looked casual, not furtive. I greeted Jonathan and even through the blood pounding in my ears I knew my voice betrayed nothing.

I was very aware, all through dinner, of Howard's attention. But it was Jean I looked at, searching for signs of strain, unhappiness, nerves. Nothing. She didn't know. She had no idea of what she was about to lose, and to whom.

When Jonathan and I left that evening Howard—as he sometimes did—gave me a brotherly kiss on the cheek. This time, though, his hand rested for a moment on my hip. No touch has ever excited me more or seemed to hold a more passionate promise.

I have been awake all night, thinking. I've been wanting this for so long, and now I can see the ending. I can have what I want, what I've always wanted. Is it enough for me to know that, or does Jean have to know, too? Do I need Howard to be happy? Or can I, now, imagine a new future for myself, without the walled garden?

The Master

THIS IS the trouble with being a newly qualified vet. The call came at 5:50 A.M. I thought it was a man's voice, though it was high for a man, and I didn't quite catch the name—Harry Sanovit? Harrison Ovett? Anyway, he said it was urgent.

Accordingly, I found myself on the edge of a plain, facing a dark fir forest. It was about midmorning. The fir trees stood dark and evenly spaced, exhaling their crackling gummy scent, with vistas of trodden-looking pine needles beneath them. A wolfwood, I thought. I was sure that thought was right. The spacing of the trees was so regular that it suggested an artificial pinewood in the zoo, and there was a kind of humming, far down at the edges of the senses, as if machinery was at work sustaining a man-made environment here. The division between trees and plain was so sharp that I had some doubts that I would be able to enter the wood.

But I stepped inside with no difficulty. Under the trees it

was cooler, more strongly scented, and full of an odd kind of
depression, which made me sure that there was some sort of
danger here. I walked on the carpet of needles cautiously, relaxed but intensely afraid. There seemed to be some kind of
path winding between the straight boles and I followed it into
the heart of the wood. After a few turns, flies buzzed around
something just off the path. *Danger!* pricked out all over my
skin like sweat, but I went and looked all the same.

It was a young woman about my own age. From the flies
and the freshness, I would have said she had been killed only
hours ago. Her throat had been torn out. The expression on
her half-averted face was of sheer terror. She had glorious red
hair and was wearing what looked, improbably, to be evening
dress.

I backed away, swallowing. As I backed, something came
up beside me. I whirled around with a croak of terror.

"No need to fear," he said. "I am only the fool."

He was very tall and thin and ungainly. His feet were in big,
laced boots, jigging a silent, ingratiating dance on the pine
needles, and the rest of his clothes were dull brown and close
fitting. His huge hands came out to me placatingly. "I am
Egbert," he said. "You may call me Eggs. You will take no
harm if you stay with me." His eyes slid off mine apolo-
getically, round and blue-gray. He grinned all over his small,
inane face. Under his close crop of straw-fair hair, his face
was indeed that of a near-idiot. He did not seem to notice the
woman's corpse at all, even though he seemed to know I was
full of horror.

"What's going on here?" I asked him helplessly. "I'm a vet,
not a—not a—mortician. What animal needs me?"

He smiled seraphically at nothing over my left shoulder. "I
am only Eggs, Lady. I don't not know nothing. What you
need to do is call the Master. Then you will know."

"So where is the Master?" I said.

He looked baffled by this question. "Hereabouts," he suggested. He gave another beguiling smile, over my right shoulder this time, panting slightly. "He will come if you call him right. Will I show you the house, Lady? There are rare sights there."

"Yes, if you like," I said. Anything to get away from whatever had killed that girl. Besides, I trusted him somehow. The way he had said I would take no harm if I was with him had been said in a way I believed.

He turned and cavorted up the path ahead of me, skipping soundlessly on his great feet, waving great, gangling arms, clumsily tripping over a tree root and, even more clumsily, just saving himself. He held his head on one side and hummed as he went, happy and harmless. That is to say, harmless to me so far. Though he walked like a great, hopping puppet, those huge hands were certainly strong enough to rip a throat out.

"Who killed that girl?" I asked him. "Was it the Master?"

His head snapped around, swayingly, and he stared at me, appalled, balancing the path as though it were a tightrope. "Oh, no, Lady. The Master wouldn't not do that!" He turned sadly, almost tearfully, away.

"I'm sorry," I said.

His head bent, acknowledging that he had heard, but he continued to walk the tightrope of the path without answering, and I followed. As I did, I was aware that there was something moving among the trees to either side of us. Something softly kept pace with us there, and, I was sure, something also followed along the path behind. I did not try to see what it was. I was quite as much angry with myself as I was scared. I had let my shock at seeing that corpse get the better of my judgment. I saw I must wait to find out how the red-headed girl had gotten herself killed. Caution! I said to myself. Caution! This path was a tightrope indeed.

"Has the Master got a name?" I asked.

That puzzled Eggs. He stood balancing on the path to think.

After a moment he nodded doubtfully, shot me a shy smile over his shoulder, and walked on. No attempt to ask my name, I noticed. As if I was the only other person there and "Lady" should be enough. Which meant that the presences among the trees and behind on the path were possibly not human.

Around the next bend, I found myself facing the veranda of a chaletlike building. It looked a little as if it were made of wood, but it was no substance that I knew. Eggs tripped on the step and floundered toward the door at the back of the veranda. Before I could make more than a move to help him, he had saved himself and his great hands were groping with an incomprehensible lock on the door. The humming was more evident here. I had been hoping that what I had heard at the edge of the wood had been the flies on the corpse. It was not. Though the sound was still not much more than a vibration at the edge of the mind, I knew I had been right in my first idea. Something artificial was being maintained here, and whatever was maintaining it seemed to be under this house.

In this house, I thought, as Eggs got the door open and floundered inside ahead of me. The room we entered was full of—well, devices. The nearest thing was a great caldron, softly bubbling for no reason I could see, and giving out a gauzy violet light. The other things were arranged in ranks beyond, bewilderingly. In one place something grotesque stormed green inside a design painted on the floor; here a copper bowl smoked; there a single candle sat like something holy on a white stone; a knife suspended in air dripped gently into a jar of rainbow glass. Much of it was glass, twinkling, gleaming, chiming, under the light from the low ceiling that seemed to come from nowhere. There were no windows.

"Good heavens!" I said, disguising my dismay as amazement. "What are all these?"

Eggs grinned. "I know some. Pretty, aren't they?" He

roved, surging about, touching the edge of a pattern here, passing his huge hand though a flame or a column of smoke there, causing a shower of fleeting white stars, solemn gong notes, and a rich smell of incense. "Pretty, aren't they?" he kept repeating, and, "*Very* pretty!" as an entire fluted glass structure began to ripple and change shape at the end of the room. As it changed, the humming which was everywhere in the room changed, too. It became a purring chime, and I felt an indescribable pulling-feeling from the roots of my hair and under my skin, almost as if the glass thing was trying to change me as it changed itself.

"I should come away from that if I were you," I said as firmly and calmly as I could manage.

Eggs turned and came floundering toward me, grinning eagerly. To my relief, the sound from the glass modulated to a new kind of humming. But my relief vanished when Eggs said, "Petra knew all, before Annie tore her throat out. Do you know as much as Petra? You are clever, Lady, as well as beautiful." His eyes slid across me, respectfully. Then he turned and hung, lurching, over the caldron with the gauzy violet light. "Petra took pretty dresses from here," he said. "Would you like for me to get you a pretty dress?"

"Not at the moment, thank you," I said, trying to sound kind. As I said, Eggs was not necessarily harmless. "Show me the rest of the house," I said, to distract him.

He fell over his feet to oblige. "Come. See here." He led me to the side of the devices, where there was a clear passage and some doors. At the back of the room was another door, which slid open by itself as we came near. Eggs giggled proudly at that, as if it was his doing. Beyond was evidently a living room. The floor here was soft, carpetlike, and blue. Darker blue blocks hung about, mysteriously half a meter or so in the air. Four of them were a meter or so square. The fifth was two meters each way. They had the look of a suite of chairs and a sofa to me. A squiggly mural-thing occupied one wall and the entire end wall was window, which seemed to lead to another veranda, beyond which I could see a garden of some kind. "The room is pretty, isn't it?" Eggs asked anxiously. "I like the room."

I assured him I liked the room. This relieved him. He stumbled around a floating blue block, which was barely disturbed by his falling against it, and pressed a plate in the wall beyond. The long glass of the window slid back, leaving the room open to the veranda. He turned to me, beaming.

"Clever," I said, and made another cautious attempt to find out more. "Did Petra show you how to open that, or was it the Master?"

He was puzzled again. "I don't not know," he said, worried about it.

I gave up and suggested we go into the garden. He was pleased. We went over the veranda and down steps into a rose garden. It was an oblong shape, carved out from among the fir trees, about fifteen meters from the house to the bushy hedge at the far end. And it was as strange as everything else. The square of sky overhead was subtly the wrong color, as if you were seeing it through sunglasses. It made the color of the roses rich and too dark. I walked through it with a certainty that it was being maintained—or created—by one of the devices in that windowless room.

The roses were all standards, each planted in a little circular bed. The head of each was about level with my head. No petals fell on the gravel-seeming paths. I kept exclaiming, because these were the most perfect roses I ever saw, whether full bloom, bud, or overblown. When I saw an orange rose— the color I love most—I put my hand up cautiously to make sure that it was real. It was. While my fingers lingered on it I happened to glance at Eggs, towering over me. It was just a flick of the eyes, which I don't think he saw. He was standing there, smiling as always, staring at me intently. There was, I swear, another shape to his face and it was not the shape of an idiot. But it was not the shape of a normal man, either. It was an intent, *hunting* face.

Next moment he was surging inanely forward. "I will pick you a rose, Lady." He reached out and stumbled as he reached. His hand caught a thorn in a tumble of petals. He snatched it back with a yelp. "Oh!" he said. "It hurts!" He lifted his hand and stared at it. Blood was running down the length of his little finger.

"Suck it," I said. "Is the thorn still in it?"

"I don't know," Eggs said helplessly. Several drops of blood had fallen among the fallen petals before he took my advice and sucked the cut, noisily. As he did so, his other hand came forward to bar my way. "Stay by me, Lady," he said warningly.

I had already stopped dead. Whether they had been there all along or had been summoned, materialized, by the scent of blood, I still do not know, but they were there now, against the hedge at the end of the garden, all staring at me. Three Alsatian dogs, I told myself foolishly and knew it was nonsense as I thought it. Three of them. Three wolves. Each of them must have been, in bulk if not in height, at least as big as I was.

They were dark in the curious darkness of that garden. Their eyes were the easiest to see, light wolf-green. All of them staring at me, staring earnestly, hungrily. The smaller two were crouched in front. One of those was brindled and larger and rangier than his browner companion. And these two were only small by comparison with the great black she-wolf standing behind with slaver running from her open jaws. She was poised either to pounce or to run away. I have never seen anything more feral than that black she-wolf. But they were all feral, stiff legged, terrified, half in mind to tear my throat out, and yet they were held there for some reason, simply staring. All three were soundlessly snarling, even before I spoke.

My horror—caught from the wolves to some extent—was beyond thought and out into a dreamlike state, where I simply knew that Eggs was right when he said I would be safe with him, and so I said what the dream seemed to require. "Eggs," I said, "tell me their names."

Eggs was quite unperturbed. His hand left his mouth and pointed at the brindled wolf in front. "That one is Hugh, Lady. Theo is the one beside him. She standing at the back is Annie."

So now I knew what had torn redheaded Petra's throat out. And what kind of a woman was she, I wondered, who must have had Eggs as servant and a roomful of strange devices, and on top of this gave three wild beasts these silly names? My main thought was that I did not want my throat torn out, too. And I had been called here as a vet after all. It took quite an effort to look those three creatures over professionally, but I did so. Ribs showed under the curly brownish coat of Theo. Hugh's haunches stuck out like knives. As for Annie standing behind, her belly clung upward almost to her backbone. "When did they last eat?" I said.

Eggs smiled at me. "There is food in the forest for them, Lady."

I stared at him, but he seemed to have no idea what he was saying. It was to the wolves' credit that they did not seem to regard dead Petra as food, but from the look of them it would not be long before they did so. "Eggs," I said, "these three are starving. You and I must go back into the house and find food for them."

Eggs seemed much struck by this idea. "Clever," he said. "I am only the fool, Lady." And as I turned, gently, not to alarm the wolves, he stretched out his hands placatingly—at least, it looked placating, but it was quite near to an attempt to take hold of me, a sketch of it, as it were. That alarmed me, but I dared not show it here. The wolves' ears pricked a little as we moved off up the garden, but they did not move, to my great relief.

Back through the house Eggs led me in his lurching, puppet's gait, around the edges of the room with the devices, where the humming filled the air and still seemed to drag at me in a way I did not care for at all, to another brightly lit, windowless room on the other side. It was a kitchen-place, furnished in what seemed to be glass. Here Eggs cannoned into a glass table and stopped short, looking at me expectantly. I gazed around at glass-fronted apparatus, some of it full of crockery, some of it clearly food stores, with food heaped behind the glass, and some of it quite mysterious to me. I made for the glass cupboard full of various joints of meat. I could see they were fresh, although the thing was clearly not a refrigerator. "How do you open this?" I asked.

Eggs looked down at his great hands, planted in encircling vapor on top of the glass table. "I don't not know, Lady."

I could have shaken him. Instead I clawed at the edges of the cupboard. Nothing happened. There it was, warmish, piled with a good fifty kilograms of meat, while three starving wolves prowled outside, and nothing I could do seemed to have any effect on the smooth edge of the glass front. At length I pried my fingernails under the top edge and pulled, thinking it moved slightly.

Egg's huge hand knocked against mine, nudging me awkwardly away. "No, no, Lady. That way you'll get hurt. It is under stass-spell, see." For a moment he fumbled doubtfully at the top rim of the glass door, but, when I made a movement to come back and help, his hands suddenly moved, smoothly and surely. The thing clicked. The glass slid open downward and the smell of meat rolled out into the kitchen.

So you *do* know how to do it! I thought. And I *knew* you did! There was some hint he had given me, I knew, as I reached for the nearest joint, which I could not quite see now.

"No, *no*, Lady!" This time Eggs pushed me aside hard. He was really distressed. "Never put hand into stass-spell. It will die on you. You do this." He took up a long, shiny pair of tongs which I had not noticed because they were nested into the top of the cupboard, and grasped the nearest joint with them. "This, Lady?"

"And two more," I said. "And when did you last eat, Eggs?" He shrugged and looked at me, baffled. "Then get out those two steaks, too," I said. Eggs seemed quite puzzled, but he fetched out the meat. "Now we must find water for them as well," I said.

"But there is juice here in this corner!" Eggs objected. "See." He went to one of the mysterious fixtures and shortly came back with a sort of cardboard cup swaying in one hand, which he handed me to taste, staring eagerly while I did. "Good?" he asked.

It was some form of alcohol. "Very good," I said, "but not for wolves." It took me half an hour of patient work to persuade Eggs to fetch out a large lightweight bowl and then to manipulate a queer faucet to fill it with water. He could not see the point of it at all. I was precious near to hitting him before long. I was quite glad when he stayed behind in the kitchen to shut the cabinets and finish his cup of "juice."

The wolves had advanced down the garden. I could see their pricked ears and their eyes above the veranda boards, but they did not move when I stepped out on to the veranda. I had to make myself move with a calmness and slowness I was far from feeling. Deliberately, I dropped each joint, one by one, with a sticky thump onto the strange surface. From the size and the coarse grain of the meat, it seemed to be venison—at least, I hoped it was. Then I carefully lowered the bowl to stand at the far end of the veranda, looking all the time through my hair at the wolves. They did not move, but the open jaws of the big wolf, Annie, were dripping.

The bowl down, I backed away into the living room, where I just had to sit down on the nearest blue block. My knees gave.

They did not move for long seconds. Then all three disappeared below the veranda and I thought they must have slunk away. But the two smaller ones reappeared, suddenly, silently, as if they had materialized, at the end of the veranda beside the bowl. Tails trailing, shaking all over, they crept toward it. Both stuck their muzzles in and drank avidly. I could hear their frantic lapping. And when they raised their heads, which they both did shortly, neatly and disdainfully, I realized that one of the joints of meat had gone. The great wolf, Annie, had been and gone.

Her speed must have reassured Theo and Hugh. Both sniffed the air, then turned and trotted toward the remaining joints. Each nosed a joint. Each picked it up neatly in his jaws. Theo seemed about to jump down into the garden with his. But Hugh, to my astonishment, came straight toward the open window, evidently intending to eat on the carpet as dogs do.

He never got a chance. Theo dropped his joint and sprang at him with a snarl. There was the heavy squeak of clawed paws. Hugh sprang around, hackles rising the length of his lean, sloping back, and snarled back without dropping his portion. It was, he seemed to be saying, his own business where he went to eat. Theo, crouching, advancing on him with lowered head and white teeth showing, was clearly denying him this right. I braced myself for the fight. But at that moment, Annie reappeared, silent as ever, head and great forepaws on the edge of the veranda, and stood there, poised. Theo and Hugh vanished like smoke, running long and low to either side. Both took their food with them, to my relief. Annie dropped out of sight again. Presently there were faint, very faint, sounds of eating from below.

I went back to the glassy kitchen, where I spent the next few hours getting Eggs to eat, too. He did not seem to regard anything in the kitchen as edible. It took me a good hour to persuade him to open a vegetable cabinet and quite as long to persuade him to show me how to cook the food. If I became insistent, he said, "I don't not know, Lady," lost interest, and shuffled off to the windowless room to play with the pretty lights. That alarmed me. Every time I fetched him back, the humming chime from the glass apparatus seemed to drag at me more intensely. I tried pleading. "Eggs, I'm going to cut these yams, but I can't find a knife somehow." That worked better. Eggs would come over obliging and find me a thing like a prong and then wander off to his "juice" again. There were times when I thought we were going to have to eat everything raw.

But it got done in the end. Eggs showed me how to ignite a terrifying heat source that was totally invisible and I fried the food on it in a glass skillet. Most of the vegetables were quite strange to me, but at least the steak was recognizable. We were just sitting down on glass stools to eat it at the glass table, when a door I had not realized was there slid aside beside me. The garden was beyond. The long snout of Hugh poked through the gap. The pale eyes met mine and the wet nose quivered wistfully.

"What do you want?" I said, and I knew I had jerked with fear. It was obvious what Hugh wanted. The garden must have filled with the smell of cooking. But I had not realized that the wolves could get into the kitchen when they pleased. Trying to seem calm, I tossed Hugh some fat I'd trimmed off the steaks. He caught it neatly and, to my intense relief, backed out of the door, which closed behind him.

I was almost too shaken to eat after that, but Eggs ate his share with obvious pleasure, though he kept glancing at me as if he was afraid I would think he was making a pig of himself. It was both touching and irritating. But the food— and the "juice"—did him good. His face became pinker and he did not jig so much. I began to risk a few cautious questions. "Eggs, did Petra live in this house or just work here?"

He looked baffled. "I don't know."

"But she used the wolves to help her in her work, didn't she?" It seemed clear to me that they *must* have been laboratory animals in some way.

Eggs shifted on his stool. "I don't not know," he said unhappily.

"And did the Master help in the work, too?" I persisted.

But this was too much for Eggs. He sprang up in agitation, and, before I could stop him, he swept everything off the table into a large receptacle near the door. "I can't say!" I heard him say above the crash of breaking crockery.

After that he would listen to nothing I said. His one idea was that we must go to the living room. "To sit elegantly, Lady," he explained. "And I will bring the sweet foods and the juice to enjoy ourselves with there."

There seemed no stopping him. He surged out of the kitchen with an armload of peculiar receptacles and a round jug of "juice" balanced between those and his chin, weaving this way and that among the devices in the windowless room. These flared and flickered and the unsupported knife danced in the air as I pursued him. I felt as much as saw the fluted glass structure changing shape again. The sound of it dragged at the very roots of me.

"Eggs," I said desperately. "How do I call the Master? Please."

"I can't say," he said, reeling on into the living room.

Some enlightenment came to me. Eggs meant exactly what he said. I had noticed that when he said 'I don't *not* know,' this did not mean that he did not know: It usually seemed to be something he could not explain. Now I saw that when he said "I can't say," he meant that he was, for some reason, unable to tell me about the Master. So, I thought, struggling on against the drag of the chiming apparatus, this means I must use a little cunning to get him to tell me.

In the living room Eggs was laying out dishes of sweets and little balls of cheese near the center of the large blue sofalike block. I sat down at one end of it. Eggs promptly came and sat beside me, grinning and breathing "juice" fumes. I got up and moved to the other end of the sofa. Eggs took the hint. He stayed where he was, sighing, and poured himself another papery cup of his "juice."

"Eggs," I began. Then I noticed that the wolf, Hugh, was crouched on the veranda facing into the room, with his brindled nose on his paws and his sharp haunches outlined against the sunset roses. Beyond him were the backs of the two others, apparently asleep. Well, wolves always leave one at least of their pack on guard when they sleep. I told myself that Hugh had drawn sentry duty and went back to thinking how I could induce Eggs to tell me how to get hold of this Master. By this time I felt I would go mad unless someone explained this situation to me.

"Eggs," I began again, "when I ask you how I fetch the Master, you tell me you can't say, isn't that right?" He nodded eagerly, obligingly, and offered me a sweet. I took it. I was doing well so far. "That means that something's stopping you telling me, doesn't it?" That lost him. His eyes slid from mine. I looked where his eyes went and found that Hugh had been moving, in the unnoticed silent way a wild creature can. He was now couched right inside the room. The light feral eyes were fixed on me. Help! I thought. But I had to go on with what I was saying before Eggs's crazed mind lost it. "So I'm going to take it that when you say 'I can't say,' you mean 'Yes,' Eggs. It's going to be like a game."

Eggs's face lit up. "I like games, Lady!"

"Good," I said. "The game is called Calling-the-Master. Now I know you can't tell me direct how to call him, but the rule is that you're allowed to give me hints."

That was a mistake. "And what is the hint, Lady?" Eggs asked, in the greatest delight. "Tell me and I will give it."

"Oh—I—er—" I said. And I felt something cold gently touch my hand. I looked down to find Hugh standing by my knees. Beyond him, Theo was standing up, bristling. "What do you want now?" I said to Hugh. His eyes slid across the plates of sweets and he sighed, like a dog. "Not sweets," I said firmly. Hugh understood. He laid his long head on my knee, yearningly.

This produced a snarl from Theo out on the veranda. It sounded like pure jealousy.

"You can come in, too, if you want, Theo," I said hastily. Theo gave no sign of understanding, but when I next looked he was half across the threshold. He was crouched, not lying. His hackles were up and his eyes glared at Hugh. Hugh's eyes moved to see where he was, but he did not raise his chin from my knee.

All this so unnerved me that I tried to explain what a hint was by telling Eggs a story. I should have known better. "In this story," I said, absently stroking Hugh's head as if he were my dog. Theo instantly rose to his feet with the lips of his muzzle back and his ears up. I removed my hand—but quick! "In this story," I said. Theo lay down again, but now it was me he was glaring at. "A lady was left three boxes by her father, one box gold, one silver, and one lead. In one of the boxes there was a picture of her. Her father's orders were that the man who guessed which of the three boxes her picture was in could marry her—"

Eggs bounced up with a triumphant laugh. "I know! It was in the lead box! Lead protects. I can marry her!" He rolled about in delight. "Are you that lady?" he asked eagerly.

I suppressed a strong need to run about screaming. I was sure that if I did, either Theo or Annie would go for me. I was not sure about Hugh. He seemed to have been a house pet. "Right," I said. "It *was* in the lead box, Eggs. This *other* lady knew that, but the men who wanted to marry her had to guess. All of them guessed wrong, until one day a beautiful man came along whom this *other* lady wanted to marry. So what did she do?"

"Told him," said Eggs.

"No, she was forbidden to do that," I said. *God give me patience!* "Just like you. She had to give the man hints instead.

Just like you. Before he came to choose the box, she got people to sing him a song and—remember, it was the *lead* box—every line in that song rhymed with "lead." A rhyme is a word that sounds the same," I added hurriedly, seeing bewilderment cloud in Eggs's face. "You know—'said' and 'bled' and 'red' all rhyme with 'lead.'"

"Said, bled, red," Eggs repeated, quite lost.

"Dead, head," I said. Hugh's cold nose nudged my hand again. Wolves are not usually scavengers, unless in dire need, but I thought cheese would not hurt him. I passed him a round to keep him quiet.

Theo sprang up savagely and came half across the room. At the same instant, Eggs grasped what a rhyme was. "Fed, instead, bed, wed!" he shouted, rolling about with glee. I stared into Theo's gray-green glare and at his pleated lip showing the fangs beneath it, and prayed to heaven. Very slowly and carefully, I rolled a piece of cheese off the sofa toward him. Theo swung away from it and stalked back to the window. "My hint is bedspread, Lady!" Eggs shouted.

Hugh, meanwhile, calmly took his cheese as deftly and gently as any hunting dog and sprang up onto the sofa beside me, where he stood with his head down, chewing with small bites to make the cheese last. "Now you've done it, Hugh!" I said, looking nervously at Theo's raked-up back and at the sharp outline of Annie beyond him.

"Thread, head, watershed, bread!" bawled Eggs. I realized he was drunk. His face was flushed and his eyes glittered. He had been putting back quantities of "juice" ever since he first showed me the kitchen. "Do I get to marry you now, Lady?" he asked soulfully.

Before I could think what to reply, Hugh moved across like lightning and bit Eggs on his nearest large folded knee. He jumped clear even quicker, as Eggs surged to his feet, and streaked off to join Theo on the veranda. I heard Theo snap at him.

Eggs took an uncertain step that way, then put his hand to his face. "What is this?" he said. "This room is chasing its tail." It was clear the "juice" had caught up with him.

"I think you're drunk," I said.

"Drink," said Eggs. "I must get a drink from the faucet. I am dying. It is worse than being remade." And he went blundering and crashing off into the windowless room.

I jumped up and went after him, sure that he would do untold damage bumping into caldron or candle. But he wove his way through the medley of displays as only a drunk man can, avoiding each one by a miracle, and reached the kitchen when I was only halfway through the room. The hum of the crystal apparatus held me back. It dragged at my very skin. I had still only reached the caldron when there was an appalling splintering crash from the kitchen, followed by a hoarse male scream.

I do not remember how I got to the kitchen. I only remember standing in the doorway, looking at Eggs kneeling in the remains of the glass table. He was clutching at his left arm with his right hand. Blood was pulsing steadily between his long fingers and making a pool on the glass-littered floor. The face he turned to me was so white that he looked as if he were wearing greasepaint. "What will you do, Lady?" he said.

Do? I thought. I'm a vet. I can't be expected to deal with humans! "For goodness sake, Eggs," I snapped at him. "Stop this messing about and get me the Master! Now. This instant!"

I think he said, "And I thought you'd never tell me!" But his voice was so far from human by then it was hard to be sure. His body boiled about on the floor, surging and seething and changing color. In next to a second the thing on the floor was a huge gray wolf, with its back arched and its jaws wide in agony, pumping blood from a severed artery in its left foreleg.

At least I knew what to do with that. But before I could move, the door to the outside slid open to let in the great head and shoulders of Annie. I backed away. The look in those light, blazing eyes said: "You are not taking my mate like *she* did."

———

HERE THE chiming got into my head and proved to be the ringing of the telephone. My bedside clock said 5:55 A.M. I was quite glad to be rid of that dream as I fumbled the telephone up in the dark. "Yes?" I said, hoping I sounded as sleepy as I felt.

The voice was a light, high one, possibly a man's. "You won't know me," it said. "My name's Harrison Ovett and I'm in charge of an experimental project involving wild animals. We have a bit of an emergency on here. One of the wolves seems to be in quite a bad way. I'm sorry to call you out at such an hour, but—"

"It's my job," I said, too sleepy to be more than proud of the professional touch. "Where are you? How do I get to your project?"

I think he hesitated slightly. "It's a bit complicated to explain," he said. "Suppose I come and pick you up? I'll be outside in twenty minutes."

"Right," I said. And it was not until I put the phone down that I remembered my dream. The name was the same, I swear. I would equally swear to the voice. This is why I have spent the last twenty minutes feverishly dictating this account of my dream. If I get back safely, I'll erase it. But if I don't— well, I am not sure what anyone can do if Annie's torn my throat out, but at least someone will know what became of me. Besides, they say forewarned is forearmed. I have some idea what to expect.

MARY   RAYNER

The Vision

NICOLAS WATCHED as the shears scissored up through the sheep's chest wool right up to the neck, as if opening the front fastening of a coat. The old man leaned over the animal to cut the wool off the back legs, where it hung over, and then the front. With a deft movement he turned the sheep onto its backside and clipped up one side just over the backbone. Then he twisted it to finish the other side. The fleece came clear off in one piece, and wordlessly he handed it to Nicolas.

The sheep righted itself with a bound and cantered over to join its fellows on the far side of the field. Nicolas took the still-warm fleece and tied it in a bundle, stacking it carefully beside the others. Fifteen now and five-and-twenty more to do. It was going well. Nicolas felt his spirits lift. It was good to be here, away for a short while from the Abbey and the endless singing. He checked himself; that was a wicked and undisciplined thought. He would have to confess it when he returned.

There were many things that Nicolas had found hard when his father had sent him to the Abbey to become a young monk, but the singing was the hardest. It was nothing like the simple tunes that he had heard around his father's farm. He had had to learn to sing the long, plaintive chants with his fellow novices, and since they were all singing the same line of melody, any wrong note was at once noticed. Over and over again Nicolas had been corrected with the rod in front of the brothers, and still he often found himself making mistakes. The worst time had been when his voice was breaking, for even when he was sure of the tune he could not be sure of his voice.

But today was different. No singing today. Now there were to be two or three days of blessed relief. He had been sent to help with the sheep shearing, oversee old Simon, and make sure that the fleeces were delivered safely back to the Abbey, that none went unaccountably missing.

The old shepherd sat down on the shearing platform and poured himself a cup of sack from the jug. "'Tis hot work," he said, smiling at the young priest and wiping his mouth with the back of his hand. "Yur, dost thee want fer to try?" He held out the shears.

Nicolas shook his head doubtfully. He had been too small when he'd left home to handle a fully grown sheep.

"Come on, I'll larn thee," said the old man. "'Twill be a durn zight more use to thee than all that there dronin' and hollerin' in the Abbey Church."

Nicolas started at hearing his own thoughts so accurately echoed. The old man shook his head, the drink making him speak freely. "I tell 'ee, 'twadden like this in the old days. I mind when all the brothers would've bin here, with their 'abits rolled up and 'elpin', but not now. Rich they be, and payin' others to do their work. 'Tis said the Abbot do keep a fine kitchen and do care more fur buildin' 'is new palace than fur rebuildin' the Abbey Church."

"'Tis not so," said Nicolas, but he wondered if it wasn't in part true. The land on which they stood belonged to the Abbey, and farms and fields for miles about. He smiled suddenly at the old man, remembering St. Benedict's motto, *Laborare est orare,* To work is to pray, and took the shears.

"Virst yer takes the fore end, zee," said the old shepherd. Nicolas cut upward over the sheep's chest as he had seen the old man do. The shears were remarkably sharp, though stiff to work. He could feel the effort needed in his wrist. He succeeded in clipping the loose wool off the back and front legs, but when he had to turn the sheep over it struggled under his uncertain grasp.

"Gently thur," said the old boy. "Her knows thee bist in a flummox." Sweat poured down Nicolas's forehead and drenched his back under the thick brown robe. He took hold of the ewe again and turned her onto her back, clipping up the side as fast as he could. The sheep lay there still enough, regarding him through wide eyes, but the shears cut into skin and a circle of scarlet spread outward in the yellowish wool.

"Thur now, look what thee's done," said the old shepherd. "Never thee mind, 'tis but a start." He moved alongside Nicolas to take the shears and finish the job off. When the sheep was on her feet again he leaned over to examine the cut. "Tidden that bad," he said. "Thur, boy, doan' be afeard. Thee canst say 'twas old Simon had had one too many sips from the jug. After all 'tis midsummer day today in this year of Our Lord twelve hundred four score and seven, and if a body can't have zummat to drink this day, then I doan' know what the world be comin' to. Take the fleece down to the stream and wash'n out, now, afore it sets." He gave the ewe a pat on her rump and she trotted off across the field, apparently none the worse. The unshorn flock bleated from their wattle enclosure as she went.

Nicolas took the fleece and walked off across the field down to the stream. Flies buzzed about him, following him in a cloud. Along the bank the ground was rutted where animals had been down to drink, and his sandaled feet slipped sideways over the dried ridges. He bent down and rinsed the blood from the wool. The sheep had all been washed before the shearing, so that the fleece was less oily than it would naturally have been, and when he lifted the wet part out of the water it hung heavy on his arm. He marched back up the field toward old Simon on his shearing platform, determined to do better next time.

All that afternoon and evening they worked, Simon doing most of the shearing, Nicolas separating out the animals, bundling up the fleeces, and now and then taking his turn with the clippers. At last, late into the evening, with the sun down and the light going fast, and a thin, white wraith of mist rising over the stream, the old shepherd took a final swill from the jug and set off across the field toward the farmstead. Nicolas took the last bundle of fleeces and bore them over to the wooden barn in the corner of the field. It was seven miles to the Abbey; no sense in going back for the night. He would sleep in the barn and be ready at daybreak to carry on.

A batch of sheep for tomorrow's shearing was penned at the far end of the barn. He undid two of the fleeces and spread them out on the beaten floor by the door; then he curled up, bone-weary, to sleep.

=====

THE FIRST thing he heard when he came to was the drumming of the rain. All about him was black dark, and for a few moments he could not recall where he was. Used as he was to waking at four in the morning for the first office of the day, he feared at first that he had slept too late and missed it, for he could not hear the usual sounds of the other brothers waking in the dormitory at the Abbey. The rain was making a curious sound, as if falling on taut cloth or leather, not on the thatch of the barn roof. He lay still, listening, as gradually it eased and then stopped.

He put a hand out in the dark and felt the mud floor beside him sodden with water. He must have rolled off the fleeces; he could not feel them anywhere. He knelt up and felt about, and could not find any of them.

Panic rose in him. Had some thief come into the barn in the night and taken them? By now his eyes were becoming accustomed to the gloom and could just make out a triangle of gray. He crawled toward it and found an opening through which he emerged onto wet grass.

And then he caught his breath in a gasp of astonishment. All about him were a hundred small points of light, flares and little fires, and rising from them a haze of smoke. Peering through the haze, he could see that the entire field was filled with brightly colored square or triangular dwellings, the tents of some mighty army, so closely packed together that the spaces in between were crisscrossed with ropes.

Nicolas drew back into the opening through which he had just crawled and pulled up the hood of his robe for warmth. The thatched barn was not there; he seemed to be inside a similar kind of tent, and water was still dripping off down the sides on to the grass. Curiously, he felt no fear now, only a kind of inquisitiveness. The soldiers of this army were wandering about in an unconcerned and unguarded way, shouting at each other cheerfully. Nicolas watched as one group gathered around a fire and pulled a pot of something on it, beginning to eat from the pot.

Another lot flung themselves down and one, seated well back under a sheltering flap of roof, began to play a stringed instrument the like of which Nicolas had never seen. It was difficult to be sure in the half light, but all seemed to be dressed in a kind of uniform; certainly the overgarments differed, but they seemed to end in the area of the waist or hips, and below all wore the same sort of leggings, most of a kind of bluish gray. All were young, and not one was bearded, Nicolas observed. He would have judged them to be somewhere about his own age, maybe a mite older. Perhaps the more seasoned campaigners were in some other encampment.

On a sudden impulse Nicolas stood up and picked his way between the tents up the field, in a direction away from the stream. Behind him the instrument player had started to sing, a tune which reminded Nicolas more of the songs of his childhood than of the plainsong of the Abbey. It was agreeable, with a catchy rhythm, and Nicolas had to stop himself humming to it.

He lifted his head and stared up the valley. Ahead of him, and to his right and his left up the sides of the hills, he could see field after field covered in more tents and brightly colored carts. Some had banners outside them with various signs drawn upon them. Perhaps there was to be some great tourney upon the morrow? He had never in all his life seen such a multitude gathered in one place. There were more here than in all the Abbey and its town, more than had ever gathered for the autumn fair at the Tor. He had no idea there were so many people in the world. He stopped and wheeled about, gasping at the size of the encampment. Here and there among the smaller tents was a larger white one, and on the far side of some open ground there seemed to be several market streets with tents and carts drawn up, forming booths from which food was being sold. There were more and brighter lights inside the booths—merchants plying their trade in the middle of the night. Nicolas was astonished.

He turned and began to walk back and saw now what he had not at first noticed, a tall, imposing structure made of shining metal supported upon rafters, its roof rising to a point, the whole of the front open to the night sky. Just below the point was an emblem, a wheel with three spokes, and on either side of the structure was a vast black coffer. Nicolas crossed himself. This must be where the leader of the army would be found, maybe a vantage point from which he could review his army.

Suddenly the dark sky was sliced by a green beam of light, traveling up and out of sight into the night. Another beam flashed across, making a different pattern. And as Nicolas watched, a group of troubadours moved onto the dais inside the structure and struck a chord on their instruments. The music was incredibly loud, and now a man's voice joined in, a voice of enormous strength and power, louder than any Nicolas had ever heard. He scanned the musicians to find the giant who produced such a voice, but the singer looked to be no bigger than average. How he could roar so loud Nicolas did not know.

Nicolas moved down the field nearer and saw that in front of the singer was a crowd, some standing, some seated, and in the midst of the crowd was a raised platform with a roof held up by scaffolding, where there seemed to be a kind of bench with figures standing beside it. One or two of the nearer bystanders turned to stare at Nicolas, and he seated himself so as to be less conspicuous. The ground was covered in straw, but even so there was mud everywhere, and rubbish and flattened cylinders of metal scattered about. Most of the crowd had their heads turned toward the dais, but of any kind of leader there seemed to be no sign.

The music roared and banged like a mighty thunderstorm, like the breakers of some vast ocean, and Nicolas felt himself lifted and flung with it, falling, tumbling headlong, and now being shaken to and fro as a dog shakes a rat. He fought its power, struggling to right himself as he felt himself sinking head downward, striking out with his left hand ineffectually over and over again, his right arm useless and pinned at his side.

And now through the noise he could hear his name being called, again and again in a man's voice, and the crowd, too, began to call out in a kind of plaintive wailing.

===

NICOLAS WOKE to find the old shepherd standing over him, shaking him by the shoulder and calling his name, while a frightened bleating was coming from the sheep at the other end of the barn. He was lying on his right arm and as he sat up he realized that his wrist was swollen and aching from the previous day's shearing. The barn was already filled with light, and the fleeces were stacked as he had left them the night before.

The old man was grumbling because it was late, but he had brought bread and a jug of milk. Nicolas wolfed both and got to his feet. He ran across the dewy grass to the stream and sluiced water over his face, still half living the extraordinary dream of the night before. He could see Simon driving the sheep from the barn to the pen near the shearing platform; it would be no use trying to tell him about it, he was anxious to start work. Nicolas offered up a prayer and strode back across the field, determined to do better than he had the day before.

All morning they labored together under the hot sun, breaking only for a hastily gulped bite and a swill of water taken from the stream. As the day wore on, they finished with the batch of sheep they had penned in the barn the night before and took a break before climbing the side of the valley to fetch the next lot down. Nicolas flung himself exhausted on the grass and the old shepherd leaned across and slapped his knee. "Thur," he said, grinning. "Us'll make a shepherd of 'ee yet, Brother Nicolas."

Halfway through the afternoon a rider appeared, coming from the direction of the village of Pilton. It was Brother Walter from the Abbey, mounted upon a pack pony. Nicolas was to return with the fleeces that had already been done, leaving Brother Walter to take over, and then come back again next day with the pony for more.

Nicolas made the long, hot journey back to the monastery with foreboding. He would have to describe his vision in confession; he could not keep it to himself. Anxiously he sought out the confessional once he had stabled the pony and handed over the fleeces, and began to recount his dream. It was as he had feared and worse.

"This is a vision sent by the Devil," said his confessor. "You say that the shepherd had a jug from which he drank. Did you, too, partake of that drink?"

Nicolas denied it. He did not know how to convey the feeling which he had had in the dream, the lack of fear, the sense of friendship and belonging which had continued right up until the last deafening storm, which had turned out to be Simon shouting at him. "They were good folk in my dream," he said. "I am sure of it."

"The Devil sends such feelings to trick us," said his confessor. "You have told me of the insignia on the leader's pavilion but of no visible leader. Is not this the mark of the Prince of Darkness? Is it not he who is the invisible leader? You have described flares and fires in the dark, and green lights, and strange loud singing. You have spoken of a multitude greater than all Christendom. Was this not a vision of Hell, my son, of the Day of Judgment?"

Nicolas frowned as he tried to concentrate his thoughts. He felt muddled and unsure of himself, but he shook his head mulishly. "No," he said, "it wasn't. They were all just singing and making music; there was a feeling of peace and friendship."

"And what was the music that these people made?" asked the confessor. "Was it the good singing that we offer up to God in the Church of St. Peter and St. Paul, or was it music made with drums and stringed instruments such as the wandering troubadours make, which as you well know is evil in the sight of God?"

Nicolas was silent. In truth it had been neither, but he knew that he could not supply an answer that would satisfy his listener. There was a long pause, and then, "Describe the folk," said the confessor.

Nicolas began on the blue leggings, on the beardless faces, on the high voices and long hair of some of the soldiers.

"I thought as much," said his interlocutor with relish. "Women! Did it not occur to you, my son, that the beardless ones with the long hair might be the daughters of Eve? Where an army goes, there, too, are to be found the temptresses of the flesh. You have been harboring unclean thoughts, my son.''

Nicolas was astonished. No, he thought wearily, it had not occurred to him. He had never seen women clad in leggings— boots too even, he could recall, now that he thought back.

His confessor was concerned by the strength of Nicolas's conviction. He was told that he should go, before absolution could be pronounced, and tell the Abbot what he thought he had seen.

The Abbot was a practical man. Privately he concluded that Nicholas had shared the contents of Simon's jug, but he ordered him to leave the monastery at first light the next day and journey back to Pilton as a penance, on foot, leading the pony. In that way he hoped that no one else in the Abbey would hear of this dream, and by the time the young man returned, the vividness of what he had seen would have faded.

Nicolas arrived back in the valley at midmorning to find Brother Walter and the old shepherd working in tight-lipped silence. It seemed that Brother Walter had issued orders to Simon on how to handle a sheep, a mistake which nothing could now undo. It was with obvious relief that Brother Walter mounted the pony to go back. ''I shall tell them to let you stay here until all is done,'' he shouted over his shoulder as he trotted away up the lane.

The old man made a wordless grunt into his beard, but his meaning was plain enough. He was glad to have Nicolas back.

Once again the two of them fell into a rhythm of work. If they kept at it they could just about finish all the sheep on the farm by the following noon.

Again that night Nicolas lay down to sleep alone in the barn, but this time he knelt in the dark and prayed that he would be shown God's truth, before stretching out on the fleeces and dropping into oblivion.

NICOLAS KNEW before he opened his eyes that the vision had come again. He could hear the music through the tent canvas and smell the woodsmoke.

He felt an odd lightening of spirit. Perhaps then it was for the good, and God had answered his prayer; perhaps this was not a manifestation of the Devil. He felt courage sweep through him. This time he would question the folk, confront them, and ask them what they were about.

He opened his eyes and saw to his surprise that it was daylight. Above and around him again was the stretched leather or cloth of the tent, bright orange. He crawled across the wet muddy floor toward the opening and found that if he took hold of a metal loop down by the ground and pulled, there came an odd tearing sound and it could be opened. He stepped out onto the sodden grass.

It was all as before, but if anything muddier underfoot and even more packed with people. There was straw down now on all the roadways between the tents, and he could see that the field down toward the stream was flooded. Now that it was no longer dark he could see people and tents more clearly, and he noticed that overhead what seemed to be thick ropes were slung from one giant metal structure to another right across the valley, from which came an intermittent crackling.

Another party of musicians was standing on the dais in the silver-white metal barn with the open front, and music soon began to thud out over the crowd. There was a pause at the end of the song while one tuned his instrument, and a distant humming made Nicolas turn his head. He watched as an enormous flying dragonfly appeared out of the leaden sky, grew larger, circled the valley, and dropped down behind the metal barn. All that he felt was a kind of mild surprise. No one else seemed in the least afraid, and Nicolas took courage from his fellow onlookers.

He took a deep breath, threw back his hood, and walked bravely away from the barn, across the open ground and past the market booths toward a large white tent where a smaller crowd was gathering. He could see now that his confessor was right; there were indeed many women and girls among the crowd, also mud-spattered children in ragged clothing, and dogs.

In the back of the large white tent were several musicians and a female singer with wild dark hair. Nicolas seated himself next to a boy of about his own age with a short-cropped head. He could not help but notice that the singer was most immodestly dressed. He averted his eyes hastily and fixed them on the boy's face, smiling uncertainly.

The boy spoke and Nicolas found that although the words were strange in his ears he could understand the meaning of what was being conveyed. "Hey," said the boy. "That's great, your outfit, better than an anorak. I en't never seen one like that before."

"It is to distinguish our Order," said Nicolas. "What is this field of folk? Whence come they?" He leaned forward. He had put the question. Now it would be revealed whether the vision came from On High or from the Realms of Darkness.

"From all over," said the boy. "Not many local. Mostly from London, the North, all parts."

Nicolas frowned. This was harder than he had thought it would be. Over the boy's shoulder he could see the girl, holding out both hands in an imploring gesture and singing as if her heart was broken. He was not sure of the words she was singing, but there was not much guessing needed to know what she was asking for.

"Why're you screwing up your eyes like that?" asked the boy. "Don't you go for her?" He jerked a thumb in the girl's direction.

"No—yes—I mean, no," said Nicolas in confusion, trying to think back to what the boy had just said. "It must take many months of journeying." He paused, and then added, hoping for further clarification, "And a great devotion to your Cause."

"Not really," said the boy. "Just a day by car or bike, see."

Nicolas was silent. This was bad. Patently not possible. The Devil must be expected to lie.

"But your Cause?" he pressed on. "The purpose of your assembly? Have you sought permission from the Abbot for such a convocation? From His Majesty, the King?"

"Oh, come off it," said the boy. "What King? What Abbot? We come mostly 'cos we like the music. Don't you?"

The girl had finished her song and was kneeling now with her head thrown back in an attitude of abandon, her hands on her hips.

"I am here on the orders of the Abbot," began Nicolas, and realized as he spoke that it was not strictly true. In these fields, yes, but at this gathering, no. It was a sort of lie. Whatever else this boy might be, he was not concealing his thoughts; he was offering a straight exchange of information; he was not lying. "Yes," admitted Nicolas. "I do like it."

The boy began to laugh. "Great," he said, and then tugged at his neighbor's coat. "Hey, Jake, listen to this guy. I dunno what he's on but he's worth listenin' to."

His friend twisted around and looked at Nicolas. "Where're you from?" he asked.

"The Abbey," said Nicolas. "I am come to discover your Purpose."

"Like he said, we come for the music," said Jake. "But it's for peace, see? For no more bombs. The bands all play for half price, or for nothin' if they're sound."

"Bombs?"

"Thick, in't 'e," said Jake's friend. "Look, mate, so's there won't be no nuclear war, see? Peace among men, an' all that. Got it?"

"*Et in terra pax,*" said Nicolas slowly. "Amen." His prayer had been answered. It was a vision, a good vision. Without realizing it he repeated the last words aloud.

"A bloody wonderful vision, if you ask me," said Jake, and he nudged his friend and shook with laughter. He leaned over sideways and extracted a damp and crumpled booklet from the back pocket of his jeans. He tore off the cover. "'Ere, take it. It's all there."

Nicolas gazed at the cover uncomprehending. Not all the monastery's teaching had yet helped him to read. Nevertheless he took it and put it in the pocket of his robe.

"Okay?" said Jake. "Now shut up, 'cos I want to 'ear this one and get an eyeful of that vision over there," and he turned back to the singer and the music.

Nicolas stood up, and walked slowly back toward the orange tent in which he had found himself.

═══

THE FOLLOWING morning Nicolas woke of his own accord in the barn. This time he remembered little of the dream, but he was filled with a sense of well-being and greeted Simon with such a smile that the old man was quite surprised.

As they had foretold, the remainder of the flock took only until noon to finish. When they had done, they carried the fleeces back to the farmstead and the old shepherd harnessed a mule to the farm cart to take them all back to the monastery.

As the cart clattered through the great gateway of the Abbey, Nicolas saw Brother Walter hastening toward them. "My Lord the Abbot wishes to speak with you, Brother Nicolas."

Nicolas swung down from the cart. He put a hand on the old shepherd's sleeve. "Fare thee well," he said. "I shall ask to come back for the dipping, if I may be allowed."

Brother Walter's lips tightened. "Make haste," he said. "The Abbot is in no mood to be kept waiting."

Old Simon ignored him. "God go with 'ee, Brother Nicolas," he said. "Us'll 'ave 'ee as a shepherd yet."

Nicolas pulled down his habit as he followed Brother Walter toward the Abbot's rooms. His hands were hot and sweaty from holding the mule reins, and he wiped them as he walked, slipping them into the pockets of his robe.

The Abbot was waiting for him, standing looking across the courtyard through the great arched window. He turned as they entered, dismissing Brother Walter with a nod.

"Our reeve at Pilton has sent to ask that you may work there," he said. "It seems that you worked hard through the shearing and promise well. I shall give my permission on one condition."

"And what is that, my Lord Abbot?" asked Nicolas.

"That you dream no more dreams of the Devil," said the Abbot, "and share no more jugs with old Simon. I want no more trouble. No more lies."

Nicolas clenched his hand in anger and felt the crumpled cover in his fingers. "It was no lie," he said quietly. "'Twas a true vision. They gave me this," and he handed the paper to the Abbot.

The Abbot took it, frowning, and smoothed it out, studying it. Then he read, out loud, "Glastonbury Festival, one nine eight seven."

Urgeya's Choice

S OMETHING IN the way his father was speaking to his mother made Thanos pause. Instead of knocking at the door he leaned closer to listen.

"They should be told, warned what to expect."

"What use would it be? Urgeya made the choice. We must live by it."

"Live? Have you chosen to forget . . ."

"Hush, Cleon, they'll hear. Don't spoil this evening for them."

Thanos backed away hurriedly. When the door opened and his parents came out, he managed to look as if he'd just entered the hall. Dorcis smiled at her son.

"Have your guests arrived yet, Thanos?"

"Yes. Zoe is with them."

"Good." She smoothed out a crease in his new tunic. "We will greet them and then leave you to play host and hostess."

96

"Not play," said Cleon. "They aren't children anymore."

Zoe was sitting on one of the two couches that flanked the dining table. Even in her new red dress she looked like a pallid version of her twin brother. The wheat gold of Thanos's hair had faded to husk brown in her. Thanos's eyes were a definite summer sky blue; hers were as colorless as rain. On either side of Zoe sat her two guests: Phyllis, plump and blonde and wearing too much jewelry, and thin, sallow Thalia, talking in her usual rapid whisper. On the opposite side of the table were the two boys. Lysis was already nibbling at a few grapes, but he jumped up when Thanos came back into the room with his parents. Dion stayed where he was, sprawling against the cushions.

"Welcome, all of you," said Cleon. "The torchbearers will come at midnight to escort you home. Until then this house is yours."

"Enjoy your feast, my dears," murmured Dorcis.

The slaves had laid out the meal just before leaving. There were cheeses and a great platter of honey cakes. Three silver flagons, two of wine and one of water, stood in front of Thanos's place. His father laid a hand on his shoulder.

"Be careful how much you drink of that wine. It's our best and stronger than you're used to."

Thanos scowled and his mother said quickly, "I know they'll be sensible."

"Do you?"

Surprised at the bitterness in her father's voice, Zoe looked up at her parents.

"Now, you remember what to do, Zoe?" her mother was saying. "Make your offerings before you go to bed and don't leave any lamps burning. The shawls . . ."

"I remember everything," said Zoe, and twisted around to reach out to Dorcis, who stooped to kiss her on the lips. Thanos hoped that she wasn't going to kiss him in front of the others, but when Dorcis reached his side of the table she just brushed his cheek with the tip of her fingers.

"Good night, Thanos. We'll be back not long after dawn."

His father stared at him for a moment and then walked out of the room without a word.

As soon as his parents had gone, Thanos said, "I am your host tonight. That means we can do what we like instead of what we're told. So first, let's change places. You girls come over here and Dion and Lysis can sit next to Zoe."

The exchange was accompanied by giggles from Phyllis and whispered protests from Thalia. Zoe began to carve slices of lamb, but Phyllis declared, "If we can do what we like, I'm going to start with what I like best—honey cakes."

"We can all see that you like sweet things best," said Thanos, pinching Phyllis's plump arm.

"Beast!"

Phyllis took a handful of honey cakes while Thanos poured three half cups of wine. He passed them to the girls and then pushed the water flagon toward them.

"You can water your wine. We'll have ours neat."

"Do you think you should?"

"I've just said what I think, Thalia. You don't have to copy us."

"I shall put plenty of water in mine," said Phyllis, tilting the jug. "All wine tastes nasty to me."

Thalia diluted her wine, too, but Zoe shook her head.

"I'll drink what Thanos does."

Her twin gave her the special smile that only passed between the two of them.

For some minutes they concentrated on eating and drinking; then Lysis couldn't wait any longer to mention the thing they were all thinking about.

"Will you go to bed or wait up?"

Phyllis waved a hand at the platters of food and the wine jugs. "After all this, if you once lie down you're bound to fall asleep."

"And dream about the Sisters," said Thanos.

"Do you think they only come in dreams?" asked Thalia.

"I don't think they come at all," declared Dion. "It's just a story adults tell to scare us, a trick to help them treat us like children. I wager tomorrow your parents will let you in on the joke and then swear you to secrecy."

"Oh, if it is a joke you will tell us, won't you?" whispered Thalia.

Thanos tilted his wine cup, first one way and then the other.

"Perhaps. But things will be different tomorrow. I'll be a man and Zoe will be a woman."

"Just because you'll be sixteen first, that doesn't make you better than the rest of us," protested Phyllis. "It's only a few months' difference."

"Only three weeks in my case," said Dion. "I'll wager my best saddle against your new dagger that it's all a joke."

"I don't need another saddle." Thanos lifted one of the silver jugs. "Your cup's empty."

He poured out more wine for all of them except Thalia, who covered her cup with one hand.

"I don't think I should. Your father did warn us not to have too much."

"Perhaps Father said that about the wine because he wanted us to get drunk," suggested Zoe.

"Wine can make you think you see all sorts of things," put in Lysis. "The first time my older brother got really drunk he saw snakes coming out of the walls."

"That wasn't what I meant."

"When it was my brother's time," began Phyllis, "he went to bed with balls of wax stuffed in his ears and swore he was going to stay under the bedclothes all night."

"What happened?"

"He wouldn't say. Nothing, I expect. He snores like a pig so he probably frightened the Sisters away."

Phyllis giggled at her own joke and took another honey cake. Lysis bit into a plump fig.

"If your monkey was here he'd be stealing these, Zoe. Did the servants take him away?"

"Yes. All the animals have gone. Even the watchdog."

"Aren't you afraid of robbers breaking in?" asked Thalia.

"Of course she isn't," exclaimed Lysis. "She's got Thanos to protect her."

"And his new dagger," murmured Dion.

"Well, I think you're very lucky to be able to wait together," said Phyllis.

"Yes," agreed Dion, "and in a comfortable bedroom in your own home, too. My mother was careless enough to have me on the roadside."

"What, not even indoors?"

"Almost on the roadside," amended Dion. "In some dirty little tavern. So that's where I'll be spending my birthnight. I hope the Sisters can drink bad wine."

"You shouldn't mock at the Mysteries," said Thalia in a shocked whisper.

"Why, what do you think will happen? Will the shadows creep up on me? Will the darkness eat me alive?"

"Don't!" said Zoe.

"What, you, too?" Dion squeezed her arm. "I'll apologize by drinking to the Sisters in this excellent wine."

"We all will." Thanos jumped to his feet and raised his cup. "To the Sisters of Night!"

They drank the toast and upended the cups to give the Sisters their share. Zoe watched the pools of wine sink into the beaten earth floor, leaving stains that were more black than red. She wondered if the wine was staining her inside, staining her black as night.

"Come on, all of you," Thanos was saying. "Eat, drink!"

Zoe shook her head to clear the wine fumes and carved slices of meat with a slightly unsteady hand. For a time there was more eating and drinking than talk.

Then, as Lysis helped himself to a whole pigeon, he asked, "What do you really think will happen, Thanos?"

"Something. I know it isn't just a joke. I overheard my parents arguing about tonight. They were serious."

"They were frightened," said Zoe. "Frightened for us."

Thanos laughed.

"Parents are always frightened about something. Frightened I'll fall off my horse, frightened I'll cut myself on my own dagger. I'm not frightened of the Sisters."

"I shan't be, either," announced Phyllis. "I'll be too curious to hear what they say."

"I don't want to know my future," said Thalia. "It might be something horrible."

Phyllis made a face.

"You're such a coward, Thalia."

"What do you want to hear, Thanos?" asked Lysis.

"Oh, I agree with Thalia."

"But you said you weren't afraid."

"I'm not afraid, but I don't want to know exactly what's going to happen to me. That would take all the excitement out of life."

"I think I'd rather know," said Lysis. "At least about when I'm going to die. So I had, well, time to get used to it."

Thalia flinched at the word "die," and Zoe said quickly, "Just because the Sisters know our futures, it doesn't mean they'll tell us about them."

"What else would they come for?" demanded Phyllis.

"I don't know," answered Zoe. "No one will tell us."

A brief silence was broken by the rattle of Phyllis's bracelets as she reached for the last of the honey cakes.

"If the Sisters do speak to you I expect it will be some boring prophecy about the war, not anything interesting like who you're going to marry."

She smiled sidelong at Thanos, but his attention was on Dion, who was demanding, "Have you heard the latest news? Another battle lost through sheer stupidity. I don't know how our parents have the face to tell us what to do when they've made such a mess of everything they're in charge of."

"And will things be so very different when you're in charge, Dion?" asked Phyllis sweetly.

"Yes, they will. In future—"

"If the Sisters know our future now," broke in Phyllis, "everything must have been decided already, so we don't have any say."

"What use is living," asked Thanos, "if we can't make our own choices?"

Zoe noticed that Lysis had gone very quiet and had even stopped eating.

"Are you all right, Lysis?"

"I think . . . I think I'm going to be sick."

They just managed to get him out into the courtyard in time. Lysis dropped to his knees and was sick all over a rosemary bush. Zoe handed him a napkin she'd snatched up from the table.

"Your guts can't keep up with your greed," murmured Dion.

"Don't mind him," said Thanos. "You'll probably feel better tomorrow than the rest of us will."

Thalia was glancing at the small altar on one side of the courtyard.

"You oughtn't to be sick in front of Urgeya. It's disrespectful."

"I couldn't help it!" gasped Lysis.

"It's time to make our offerings, anyway," said Thanos. "That should placate her."

"Everyone fetch some food from the table," ordered Zoe. "No, not you, Lysis. I'll bring some grapes for you to give."

When each of them was equipped with an offering, they approached the altar and the statue in the niche above. The dumpy, olive-wood figure of Urgeya was so worn you could hardly see it was meant to be a woman. Zoe had always enjoyed touching its smooth curves, but while she looked at the statue the features seemed to melt, as if Urgeya was retreating deep into the wood. No! Don't you leave, thought Zoe. Not you as well.

Thanos nudged her arm.

"Go on."

Zoe held up a small loaf of poppy bread.

"Lady Urgeya, Mother of Our People. Zoe and Thanos bring you offerings on their birthnight."

She put the loaf at the statue's feet, and Thanos poured half a jug of wine over the altar.

"Our friends, Thalia and Phyllis and Dion and Lysis, who have shared our birthnight feast, also bring you offerings. Lady Urgeya, please take these gifts."

Dion whispered something in Phyllis's ear. Thalia scowled at them both. When all the offerings were in place, Zoe spoke again. "Please protect us through this night. Don't leave us here alone."

A sudden crash seemed like an angry refusal of her plea.

"Don't tremble like that," said Thanos. "It's only the torchbearers knocking."

The twins stood in the street to say good night to their guests. Phyllis was the last to leave. As she hugged Zoe she whispered, "Promise you'll tell me what it's like?"

Zoe returned the hug but didn't speak. She and Thanos walked back into the house together. Thanos barred the door and then damped down the fires while Zoe went around blowing out the lamps. The remains of their feast would lie on the table until morning. They ignored the doors to their own bedrooms and went into their parents' room. Across the wide bed were stretched two linen shawls.

"You're not going to lie down, are you?"

When Zoe shook her head, Thanos picked up the shawls and tossed the left-hand one to her. She stretched it taut in her hands, looking at the small, neat repairs in the fragile cloth. Then she put the shawl around her shoulders, the shawl she had been wrapped in as a newborn baby sixteen years ago to the night. Thanos knotted his shawl around his hips and wandered about picking things up. It seemed odd to be alone in this room, free to be as curious as they liked about their parents' possessions.

"Father was born here, too, wasn't he?" asked Zoe.

"Yes." Thanos lifted the lid of a chest and drew out one of his father's cloaks. "He must have waited here on his birth-night just like us."

"But alone."

Zoe tried to imagine how her father would have felt, while Thanos crossed to a small table and picked up his mother's comb and looked into a box which held earrings.

"There was a war even then," murmured Zoe. "Though not the same one, of course. I remember the day this war started. We were five. Father came in and forgot to kiss me. I knew something bad must have happened. I thought it was my fault so I started to cry."

"And I hit father for making you cry."

"And mother slapped you and then started crying, too. Do you remember the time the news came that Cousin Xeno had been killed? I thought of him as so grown-up, but he can't have been that much older than we are now."

"Stop looking back!" exclaimed Thanos. "That's for old people, people who've come to the end of things. Tonight is where we begin."

"Then put out the lamps," said Zoe.

Thanos reached up to pinch out the wick in the metal lamp that hung from the ceiling but seemed reluctant to blow out the small terra-cotta lamp that stood by the bed. He picked it up and cradled its warmth for a moment.

"You do it, Zoe."

She leaned forward, blowing hard, and the small flame died. There was still a little light from the moon filtering in through the grill on the only window. They sat down cross-legged in front of the cold hearth. Zoe shivered and pulled her shawl tighter across her shoulders.

"I wish we could light the fire."

They sat without talking for a while. How quiet the house is, thought Zoe. She'd never realized before how the night was made friendly by the faint noises of people and animals sleeping all around her. Now they were missing, her home seemed a different place. Everything was strange to her, even her own body. She wondered for a moment if she was going to be sick like Lysis, but the nausea didn't seem to be coming from inside her. It was a pressure from outside, as if she was trapped in the center of a tightening ring of silence. She was sure that Thanos could feel it, too.

"Do you think we just wait or can we call them?"

"Let's try calling them," said Thanos, gratefully.

He got to his knees.

"Sisters of Night, come to us! This is our birthnight. We are waiting for you. Waiting to hear our fate. Sisters of Night, come to us!"

He repeated the invocation seven times but no answer came. Silence reclaimed the room. The moon was masked by clouds and the darkness deepened.

After a few minutes Thanos said, "Perhaps they won't come until the exact moment we were born."

"You were born half an hour before I was. Suppose you see them before I can? We'll each be alone with them after all!"

Thanos took her hand.

"We're twins. We feel the same things. When I see them you will, too."

Zoe tried to smile.

"I used to look forward so much to this night. I so wanted to know what would happen, what the truth was. Now I just wish it was all over. I wish it was morning and Mother and Father were back."

"I don't," said Thanos, but he didn't let go of her hand.

Silence surrounded them again. The wine was making Zoe drowsy now. She felt that if they weren't holding hands she would drift away into sleep. She shook herself and, staring down at where the hearth must be, tried to keep awake by thinking about ordinary things: her new dress, tomorrow's breakfast, how her pet monkey must be missing her. Then the moon came out again and Thanos gripped her so hard that she started to protest. She stopped when she saw the look on her brother's face. He was staring over her shoulder at something. Very slowly Zoe turned her head.

The seven Sisters of Night were standing in a semicircle behind her. They were very tall and swathed and hooded in gray, a gray so translucent that the moonlight shone through them. Zoe wondered how long they had been standing there, motionless and silent, and then knew that they had always been present, bodiless because they were stretched across all times at once. Her tongue seemed swollen with fear, her lips too dry to speak. It was difficult even to move, but at last she managed to squeeze her brother's hand. He stirred as if she had brought him out of a trance.

"Sisters of Night . . ."

Thanos's words came out as a whisper. Zoe squeezed his hand again and he went on in a stronger voice.

"Sisters of Night. Tell us our fate."

"It is yours to choose."

One voice seemed to come from the seven unseen mouths, a voice like a cold wind rustling dead leaves. It was a moment before Zoe realized what had been said.

"M-my choice?" stammered Thanos.

"Urgeya, the Mother of her People, searched the three worlds for us. She found the Cave of the Fates and passed the grim guardians to reach us. To reward her courage we granted her one wish. She asked that all her people might be allowed to choose the length of their lives. That is the Choice of Urgeya. It is your choice now."

Zoe saw her brother's face transformed with wonder and excitement. He knelt upright, no longer afraid.

"Then everything is better than we knew! Our fates belong to us. We can choose."

"Stand up. Before you make your choice, you must come with us."

Letting go of Zoe's hand, Thanos jumped to his feet. Zoe stood up more slowly. The semicircle became a circle. The Sisters of Night surrounded them and blurred into a spinning ring of gray. As the ground seemed to rock beneath her, Zoe closed her eyes and dizzily groped for her brother's hand.

When the rocking ceased she opened her eyes again. The Sisters still stood in a circle, but with only blackness behind them their bodies seemed more solid. Zoe felt a chill striking up through her feet. They were standing on a surface as hard and cold and translucent as ice.

"Kneel and look down."

Zoe and Thanos obeyed.

At first they saw nothing but a shimmering darkness. Then the darkness resolved itself into a great black disk very far below them. Scattered across the disk were thousands upon thousands of tiny points of light, not the cold white of stars, but the warm amber of flame. Concentrating on the points of light, it seemed to Zoe that they were very frail. Hundreds flickered out while she watched, as if some great wind was sweeping across the black disk.

"Now you see your world as we see it."

"I don't understand," began Thanos.

"Watch."

Thanos bowed his head and looked down again. One of the points of light seemed to glow more brightly than the rest. Its amber was streaked with red and glittering gold that flared up to defy the darkness. The unseen wind seemed to fan the flame until it lit the whole disk and soared higher and higher. So high that Zoe thought the pillar of flame would reach them and melt the ice on which they stood. Just as Thanos gasped and Zoe shrank back, the flame collapsed in on itself and dissolved into a dazzling rain of sparks, falling to extinction. Then there was nothing but darkness and the small points of light again.

"Oh, beautiful . . . ," breathed Thanos.

"Each one of you has a soul of flame, each must choose how much of yourself to feed to that flame. If you ask for safety and long life, then the flame will barely last your years and will have no power to burn bright. If you choose danger and risk and a short life, the flame can leap high enough to light your whole world. It will reach almost to the heavens and scorch the gods."

"Yes!" Thanos was staring up at the Sisters of Night, his face ecstatic. "I choose to leap, to light up the darkness."

Zoe still saw the shower of brilliant sparks as if they had burned into her eyes. Thanos gripped her hand.

"Zoe, tell them we'll go together. The two of us in one great flame!"

Zoe looked down at the myriad tiny points of light. The points that didn't flare into brief and lonely brilliance, the points that needed each other, standing together against the great wind, enduring for as long as they could.

"No," whispered Zoe.

The amber lights were snuffed out by a grayness that seemed to fill the whole world. Though she was no longer kneeling on ice, but on the floor of her parents' bedroom, Zoe still shivered. Thanos was beside her and she watched the elation sucked from his face by returning silence. The seven Sisters of Night encircled them, waiting for one last question.

Thanos whispered: "Sisters of Night, have I . . . ?"

"You have made the Choice of Urgeya. Death for Thanos. Life for Zoe."

A sudden anger gave Zoe courage.

"It was a trick, wasn't it? Urgeya thought she was helping her people, saving us by letting us set the length of our own lives. But you knew how it would be, you knew how many young people would choose death."

She stopped because the Sisters of Night were fading, merging back into the shadows until the last thing left was the sound of their laughter. The Laughter of the Fates that meant death for Xeon, death for Thanos, death for the brightest and the best.

"Zoe?"

Thanos's voice sounded much younger to her, as if she had grown old in a night and left her twin behind.

"Zoe. It was beautiful . . . the pillar of flame. It was beautiful, wasn't it?"

"Yes, very beautiful."

Zoe held out her arms and Thanos leaned against her. How many times will I do this? thought Zoe. How many times will I be the comforter before my light flickers out?

"We won't tell anyone about tonight," said Thanos.

"No."

They sat holding each other, waiting for dawn.

H E L E N   C R E S S W E L L

The Sky Sea

You don't have to believe this story. Plenty wouldn't. I'm just telling you what happened, that's all. In fact, I may as well tell you that the main reason I'm writing it all down is in the hope that once I see it in black and white, *I* won't believe it, either. If there is one thing I don't want, it's to end up like my great-aunt Cass. I'm hoping to be a neurosurgeon.

I know perfectly well that nobody has great-aunts these days, but I did. (Past tense, you notice.) I'm an only, so when I was little my parents were always farming me out to relatives so that I'd get the feeling of belonging to a big, happy family. Some chance. All my aunts and uncles, and particularly my cousins, are horrendous. One of them even has personalized plates on his car, for heaven's sake. One of the main things I'm looking forward to about being grown-up is being able to ditch the lot of them. So it's rather sad that the one person I did like visiting was Great-Aunt Cass.

She was what my mother called "slightly dotty," but was probably just plain mad. You'll be able to make your own mind up. But the point is that when I was little, my favorite thing was going to stay with her.

She lived in a tiny village in Herefordshire called Flintham. Her house was very old and full of odd shadows and corners—rather like its owner, I suppose. It had a funny smell—of herbs, I think. She was always growing them and drying them. I used to help her, and she'd tell me what they all were and what ills they cured. I can't remember any of them and, in any case, doubt whether they'll come in for much when I'm a neurosurgeon. Anyway, she believed in them all right and used to call the local GP "Dr. Quack"—sometimes to his face. I thought it was his real name, at the time.

The minute my parents had driven off, Great-Aunt Cass would fix me with her eye and grin the wickedest grin I've ever seen on any old lady.

"Well, Daisy dear, what shall we do for treats?"

And I'd shake my head and say, "You choose," because I knew I'd never be able to think up anything half as good as what she'd come up with. A lot of her treats were to do with eats. We'd make a whole batch of macaroons or drop scones and eat the lot in a sitting. Or we'd catch a bus into Ledbury and go to this café where we'd have two cream teas each, one after the other. My parents would have gone spare if they'd known. They were keen on healthy eating as well as big families. I was only allowed one biscuit a day at home.

Then we'd go looking for watercress. Great-Aunt Cass would wear these old wellies and tuck her skirts right up, and once she even fell over in the stream and got soaked, which was marvelous. She didn't even care. She just squelched home and got changed and swallowed a great, steaming mug full of some herb tea. Most old ladies I know would have gone into a galloping decline, even supposing they'd have gone wading about looking for watercress in the first place. I don't know how old she was, but at the time I thought she must be about a hundred.

If it rained, we used to cut out these old Victorian cards and pictures she had and stick them onto cupboard doors and things as decorations. Or we'd make things she called "peas in a pod." This meant that we'd each make exactly the same thing—a cat in clay, for instance, or a cardboard stand-up doll to dress. They never came out like peas in a pod, of course, but she said it didn't matter.

"You've got one, and I've got one. It's a charm—it binds us together."

I liked the idea of that.

One day she said, "We'll make something together, and then we'll split it in half. Half for you and half for me. That will bind us even closer."

So we made a big bird, a swallow, out of clay. And while it was still soft, she cut it straight down the middle with a knife. Then when it was baked we had half each and painted it blue. She kept her half on the mantelpiece, and I took mine home and kept it by the side of my bed.

"That's *real* magic," she said.

I told you she was mad.

I can't remember exactly how old I was when she first started talking about the sea in the sky. I think I must have been around five or six. However old I was, I sure as hell believed every single word of it.

Oh, Lord. I can see that when I start telling it you're going to think I'm totally off my trolley. What you've got to remember is that although I'm fifteen now, I was only *little*. In fact, what I think I'll do, if you don't mind, is from now on tell it as if it were a story in the third person—Daisy said this, Daisy did that, and so on. That way you'll get the message that it was me then, not me now. I mean, it could just as well have happened to you. I didn't ask for it to happen; it just did.

Anyway, that's what I'll do. I may not tell it all that brilliantly—I never get all that good marks for English (unlike math, physics, biology, and chemistry, says she modestly). And from now on I'll just put GAC, instead of the whole mouthful (or penful), if you don't mind. So here goes. . . .

=====

DAISY WAS not very high and was in a forest world of gooseberries and black currants. The smell was hot and sweet and dusty all at once. Her fingers were stained with juice but not her mouth, because you couldn't eat gooseberries and black currants as fast as you picked them, as you could with raspberries and strawberries. You had to wait until they had been stewed into a lovely, sweet, sticky mixture that GAC called potpourri.

Winding in and out of the bushes was the ginger, white, and tortoiseshell cat called Porker, though nobody knew why. If GAC were ever asked she simply replied, "It suits him." The sun beat down on Daisy and her bowl was nearly full. She thought of the homemade lemonade in the pantry, in a jug covered with muslin edged with beads. (She and GAC had made one each the day before.) She pushed through the jungle of leaves and out onto the square patch of grass.

There was GAC, lying back in her chair gazing up at the sky. She didn't look at Daisy, but she must have known she was there because she said, "Did you know there's a sea up there?"

Daisy, interested, put down her bowl and tilted back her head, screwing her eyes against the sun.

"A sea with tides and waves and ships and sailors."

Daisy squinted the harder. The sky was a fierce blue and flecked with wispy clouds, like foam. She shook her head.

"That's the sky," she said. She knew that for a fact.

"And above the sky, a sea." GAC's voice was far away and dreamy. It often was. "I know. Do you believe in mermaids?"

"'Course," said Daisy promptly. It was a silly question.

"Of course. Sit here on the grass—lie down, if you like. And watch the sky—watch it very carefully."

Daisy obeyed. She lay on the hot grass and stared up, straining for a glimpse of a galleon with white sails, like the one in her nursery rhyme book. She was just on the point of thinking she saw one when she fell asleep.

"Well?" asked GAC when Daisy awoke. "Did you see anything?"

"I kind of did," replied Daisy. "Sort of."

Now she knew about the sea above the sky, she would look up at the sky from time to time and see it with new eyes. It certainly looked deep enough to hold a sea.

It might have been that night, or the night after, or even the night after that, when GAC told Daisy the story. She was always telling stories and they were marvelous ones about dragons and sorcerers and spells and they were all true.

"All the things I'm going to tell you really happened," she began that night. "And they happened many years ago, here in Flintham."

"Like the one about the man with two heads, you mean?"

"Precisely," said GAC. "Now, don't interrupt. The story begins one thick, cloudy day—a Sunday, because the people were just coming out of church. All of them were thinking about their roast dinners, I daresay, just as you or I would. And then somebody noticed an anchor hanging on one of the tombstones."

"Which one? Not the one for Daisy Martha Bell in her seventieth year, LIFE'S WORK WELL DONE?"

"Probably. It doesn't matter. The point is, anchors don't belong in churchyards, and this particular one certainly hadn't been there when they went in. They all crowded around to look and saw that the anchor was attached to a cable, and that cable was pulled tight and stretching right into the sky as far as you could see. It just hung there in the air. It had them all by their ears, I can tell you! They gabbled and gawped and couldn't think what to do. And then the rope began to jerk and tug, right under their eyes, as if someone was trying to pull it up. But the anchor was hooked fast to the tombstone and wouldn't budge.

"Far away up above, the congregation could hear voices shouting, and then they knew that up there, although it was quite impossible, was a ship, and sailors!

"And then—a sailor came sliding down the rope—"

"Out of the *sky*!"

"Out of the sky. He slid right down till he reached the ground, then seized the anchor and tugged and heaved to free it from the tombstone. But the anchor held fast. In the end he loosened it slightly, but just as he did so the villagers ran forward and seized him. They pulled him away from the anchor and held him down. After a while the sailors above must have given up hope, because the cable was cut and came spiraling down out of the sky and fell in a huge heap."

"Oh, the poor man! And he couldn't get back."

"He couldn't get back. He died. He drowned, I suppose you might say."

"Poor man, poor man!"

"And his ship in the sky went sailing away without him."

"What was it like?"

"The ship? No one knows. No one saw it."

"Perhaps there wasn't one at all."

"You can't have an anchor without a ship."

"And it's all true?"

"True as I sit here with my shoes pinching. Wait till tomorrow and I'll show you something."

The next day Daisy went with GAC to the church. Porker went paddling after them through the long grass. He always did, just like a dog. Daisy looked left and right among the barnacled tombstones for sign of an anchor.

"Not today," GAC told her. "Anchors never drop in the same place twice."

Then she led Daisy to the thick oak door of the church and pointed at the great iron hinges.

"The anchor!" she said. "The people forged those hinges out of the anchor, in memory of that amazing event."

Gingerly Daisy touched them, first one, then the other. They were cold—sea cold.

Now that she knew for certain that there was a sea above the sky, Daisy soon began to take it for granted. She even supposed that rain was that same sea, leaking. Before, she had wondered wherever it could come from. Now the world made more sense.

After that, on every visit GAC would talk about the sea in the sky. She had seen the ships, she said. They were tall masted with billowing white sails. She had heard the sailors singing aloft.

"I suppose that to them, all earth folk are mermaids," mused GAC. "You and I are mermaids, dear."

Daisy looked dubiously down at her shoes and socks, but said nothing.

Then one time—it must have been a summer or two later—GAC showed Daisy a curious curved comb, carved out of tortoiseshell. It looked very old and had a pale, misty bloom.

"I found it among the hollyhocks," she said. "It must have been dropped over the side of a ship!"

"So it must," agreed Daisy.

She ran straight into the garden to see if she could find something of her own. She poked among the pansies and delphiniums and in among the raspberry cane forest, but all she found was a rusty teaspoon.

"Mine," GAC told her. "Not old—just rusty. Never mind. Just wait."

By now Daisy was so certain that she lived at the bottom of a real sea that she half expected to see fishes fly instead of birds, coral for stones, silvery sand for earth. Ghostly galleons wove in and out of her dreams.

On Daisy's next visit GAC began to talk about going away. "It's a secret, between you and me," she told Daisy.

"You won't go forever?" Daisy didn't like people to disappear. She didn't like the way GAC disappeared between visits and would make her write letters to prove that she was still there.

"That I can't tell. I am going on a voyage."

"On a ship?"

"On a ship."

"On the sea above the sky?"

"You guessed," GAC told her.

"But how will you get up there? Will you climb up a rope?"

"I don't know that, either. But I expect the sailors will haul me up. Me and Porker."

"Porker?"

"He shall be ship's cat. He'll like it. I think he was born to be a ship's cat. Haven't you noticed the way he rolls as he goes, like a sailor?"

Daisy hadn't. She thought that Porker walked in a perfectly ordinary catlike way. If anything was strange about him, it was his name.

"My throat feels sore," she said. She said it to change the subject, because she didn't want to think about GAC and Porker sailing off in the sky, but it was true, anyway.

Soon her throat was so sore that she couldn't swallow, and her arms and legs didn't seem to want to move. She remembered being put to bed and the doctor being there. She remembered GAC wiping her face with something damp and cool, giving her something sweet and sticky, and then something cold and slippery to swallow. It was night, and the curtains were undrawn as they always were. And it was the longest and strangest night Daisy had ever known.

Afterward she could never sort out what were dreams and what were memories. All she knew was that that night both she and GAC saw a galleon sail right over the moon in a smoking sea of cloud. GAC threw open the window, and in, on the cold draft, there blew the faint and faraway shouts of sailors.

"They're there, my darling," said the voice of GAC. "Don't you hear them?"

But Daisy was herself adrift on a fathomless sea and did not answer, though she followed the wake of the ship with her eyes and thought she heard gulls crying.

Next day when she opened her eyes Daisy looked straight at the sky, but it had closed again, gone ordinary, and the ship had gone.

"You had a fever," GAC told her. "But you'll mend, and not on account of Dr. Quack, either. You can take his sticky medicine, but it's mine'll put you to rights."

So Daisy obediently swallowed both, and did mend, though she never knew which to thank.

She was still wobbly on the day she went home.

"Good-bye," said GAC. "Look out for Porker and me in the sky."

"Oh, you will come back; say you'll come back!"

"Make no promises you can't keep," replied GAC. "But I promise you one thing. I'll send you a sign. And I'll give you this to keep."

She opened her hand and there was the old, curved comb with its curious milky bloom.

"Oh, *thank* you!"

It would go beside her bed, with the blue half swallow.

"And not a word!"

"Promise!"

Daisy said good-bye to GAC and to Porker, and never saw either of them again.

"She says she's gone on a voyage," Daisy's mother said, when the letter came. "I suppose she means a cruise. At her age! Oh, well, she always was slightly dotty. Oh—and taken Porker, she says!"

"That's more than slightly dotty," said Daisy's father. "That's trouble."

"Oh, she can't possibly have taken him. They wouldn't allow it. I expect she's put him in a home."

As the weeks passed, no postcards arrived from foreign parts. Daisy, of course, did not expect any, since she thought it unlikely that there was a post office in the sky. She kept her eyes glued to that sky and sometimes wondered, when her eyes began to ache, whether perhaps this was a different sky from the one that hung over Flintham.

"We had better go over and see what's happening," Daisy's mother said one day.

The garden was already overgrown. Soon, thought Daisy, the raspberries and gooseberries and thistles would close up in a thicket, as if in a fairy tale. On the back door was pinned a note, by now faded and smudged by sun and rain. "Gone on a voyage. Don't know when I'll be back."

Inquiries were made in the village.

"Oh, yes, Miss Norton said she was going on a voyage."

"A cruise, you mean?"

"That's not what she said. She said a voyage, I'm sure. And that's what the note on her door says."

And that was that. There was nothing more to be done. And Daisy kept her secret.

———

So THERE you are. Now do you see why I wanted to tell it in the third person? It's odd—as I was telling it, it all came back very clearly—I could even smell things—the hot black currants, the warm macaroons, the scent of herbs. But Daisy Then doesn't seem to be Daisy Now at all. I can hardly believe I was her, once. Imagine believing all that guff!

The only thing is, I haven't quite told you everything. I don't really want to, but I know I must, or it would be cheating. And it's the real reason I'm telling the story at all.

It happened last week. I swear I hadn't been thinking about GAC at all. In fact, the only time I ever think of her now is when I see that half swallow and the comb. I was in the garden, revising, and absolutely *compos mentis*. Then all of a sudden, right out of the blue, I thought I heard GAC's voice, "Ahoy! Daisy!" That's all—and then a soft thud, right nearby. Believe it or not, I actually looked up at the sky, and of course there was nothing there. But then I looked down. And there, quite close by, was something blue and shiny. It was the other half of that clay swallow we'd made together that rainy day, all those years ago in Flintham.

E M M A   B U L L

A Bird That Whistles

THE DULCIMER player sat on the back steps of Orpheus Coffeehouse, lit from behind by the bulb over the door. His head hung forward, and his silhouette was sharp against the diffused glow from State Street. The dulcimer was propped against his shoulder as if it were a child he was comforting. I'd always thought you balanced a dulcimer across your knees. But it worked; this sounded like the classical guitar of dulcimer playing. Then his chin lifted a little.

> *'' 'Twas on one bright March morning, I bid New Orleans adieu,*
> *And I took the road to Jackson town, my fortunes to renew.*
> *I cursed all foreign money, no credit could I gain,*
> *Which filled my heart with longing for the lakes of Pontchartrain.''*

He got to the second verse before he stopped and looked up. Light fell on the side of his face.

"I like the bit about the alligators best," I said stupidly.

"So do I." I could hear his grin.

"'If it weren't for the alligators, I'd sleep out in the woods.' Sort of sums up life." He sounded so cheerful, it was hard to believe he'd sung those mournful words.

"You here for the open stage?" I asked. Then I remembered *I* was, and my terror came pounding back.

He lifted the shoulder that supported the dulcimer. "Maybe." He stood smoothly. I staggered up the steps with my banjo case, and he held the door for me.

In the full light of the back room his looks startled me as much as his music had. He was tall, slender, and pale. His black hair was thick and long, pulled into a careless tail at the back, except for some around his face that was too short and fell forward into his eyes. Those were the ordinary things.

His clothes were odd. This was 1970 and we all dressed the way we thought Woody Guthrie used to: blue denim and work shirts. This guy wore a white T-shirt, black corduroys, and a black leather motorcycle jacket that looked old enough to be his father's. (I would have said he was about eighteen.) The white streak in his hair was odd. His face was odd; with its high cheekbones and pointed chin, it was somewhere out beyond handsome.

But his eyes—they were like green glass, or a green pool in the shadow of trees, or a green gemstone with something moving behind it, dimly visible. Looking at them made me uncomfortable; but when he turned away, I felt the loss, as if something I wanted but couldn't name had been taken from me.

Steve O'Connell, the manager, came out of the kitchen, and the green-eyed man handed him the dulcimer. "It's good," he said. "I'd like to meet whoever made it."

Steve's harried face lit up. "My brother. I'll tell him you said so."

Steve disappeared down the hall to the front room, and the green eyes came back to my face. "I haven't forgotten your name, have I?"

"No." I put my hand out, and he shook it. "John Deacon."

"Banjo player," he added. "I'm Willy Silver. Guitar and fiddle."

"Not dulcimer?"

"Not usually. But I dabble in strings."

That's when Lisa came out of the kitchen.

Lisa waited tables at Orpheus. She looked like a dancer, all slender and small and long boned. Her hair was a cirrus cloud of red-gold curls; her eyes were big, cat tilted, and gray; and her skin was so fair you should have been able to see through it. I'd seen Waterhouse's painting *The Lady of Shalott* somewhere (though I didn't remember the name of the painter or the painting then; be kind, I was barely seventeen), and every time I saw Lisa I thought of it. She greeted me by name whenever I came to Orpheus, and smiled, and teased me. Once, when I came in with the tail end of the flu, she fussed over me so much I wondered if it was possible to get a chronic illness on purpose.

Lisa came out of the kitchen, my heart gave a great loud thump, she looked up with those big, inquiring eyes, and she saw Willy Silver. I recognized the disease that struck her down. Hadn't she already given it to me?

Willy Silver saw her, too. "Hello," he said, and looked as if he was prepared to admire any response she gave.

"Hi." The word was a little breathless gulp. "Oh, hi, John. Are you a friend of John's?" she asked Willy.

"I just met him," I told her. "Willy Silver, Lisa Amundsen. Willy's here for open stage."

He gave me a long look, but said, "If you say so."

I must have been feeling masochistic. Lisa always gets crushes on good musicians, and I already knew Willy was one. Maybe I ought to forget the music and just commit sep-puku onstage.

But you can't forget the music. Once you get the itch, it won't go away, no matter how much stage fright you have. And by the time my turn came—after a handful of guys-on-stools-with-guitars, two women who sang a cappella for too long, a woman who did Leonard Cohen songs on the not-quite-tuned piano, and the Orpheus Tin-and-Wood Toejam Jug Band—I had plenty of stage fright.

Then Willy Silver leaned over from the chair next to me and whispered, "Take your time. Play the chord progression a couple of times for an intro—it'll settle you down."

I looked up, startled. The white streak in his hair caught the light, and his eyes gleamed green. He was smiling.

"And the worst that can happen isn't very bad."

I could embarrass myself in front of Lisa . . . and everyone else, and be ashamed to ever show my face in Orpheus again. But Willy didn't look like someone who'd understand that.

My hands shook as if they had engine knock. I wanted to go to the bathroom. Steve clumped up onstage, read my name from the slip of paper in his hand, and peered out into the dark room for me. I hung the banjo over my shoulder and went up there to die for my art.

I scrapped the short opening I'd practiced and played the whole chord progression instead. The first couple mea-sures were shaky. But banjos give out a lively noise that makes you *want* to have a good time, and I could feel mine sending those messages. By the time I got around to the words, I could remember them and sing them in almost my usual voice.

> *"I got a bird that whistles, honey, got a bird,*
> *Baby, got a bird that will sing.*
> *Honey, got a bird, baby, got a bird that will sing.*
> *But if I ain't got Corinna, it just don't mean,*
> *It don't mean a natural thing."*

At the back of the room, I could just see the halo of Lisa's hair. I couldn't see her face but at least she'd stopped to listen. And down front, Willy Silver sat, looking pleased.

I did "Lady Isabel and the Elf Knight" and "Newry Highwayman." I blew some chords and forgot some words but I lived through it. And people applauded. I grinned and thanked them and stumbled off the stage.

"Do they clap because they like what you did," I asked Willy, "or because you stopped doing what they didn't?"

Willy made a muffled noise into his coffee cup.

"Pretty darn good," said Lisa, at my elbow. I felt immortal. Then I realized that she was stealing glances at Willy. "Want to order something, now that you're not too nervous to eat it?"

I blushed, but in the dark, who could tell? "PB and J," I told her.

"PB and J?" Willy repeated.

We both stared at him, but it was Lisa who said, "Peanut butter and jelly sandwich. Don't you call them that?"

The pause was so short I'm not sure I really heard it. Then he said, "I don't think I've ever been in a coffeehouse where you could order a peanut butter and jelly sandwich."

"This is it," Lisa told him. "Crunchy or smooth, whole wheat or white, grape jelly or peach preserves."

"Good grief. Crunchy, whole wheat, and peach."

"Nonconformist," she said admiringly.

He turned to me when she went toward the kitchen. "You *were* pretty good," he said. "I like the way you sing. For that last one, though, you might try mountain minor."

"What?"

He got an eager look on his face. "Come on," he said, sprang out of his chair, and led the way toward the back.

We sat on the back steps until the open stage was over, and he taught me about mountain minor tuning. His guitar was a deep-voiced old Gibson with the varnish worn off the strategic spots, and he flat-picked along with me, filling in the places that needed it. Eventually we went back inside, and he taught me about pull-offs. As Steve stacked chairs, we played "Newry Highwayman" as a duet. Then he taught me "Shady Grove," because it was mountain minor, too.

I'd worked hard at the banjo, and I enjoyed playing it. But I don't think I'd ever been aware of making something beautiful with it. That's what those two songs were. Beautiful.

And Lisa moved through the room as we played, clearing tables, watching us. Watching him. Every time I looked up, her eyes were following his face or his long fingers on the guitar neck.

I got home at two in the morning. My parents almost grounded me; I convinced them I hadn't spent the night raising hell by showing them my new banjo tricks. Or maybe it was the urgency with which I explained what I'd learned and how, and that I had to have more.

When I came back to Orpheus two nights later, Willy was there. And Lisa, fair and graceful, was often near him, often smiled at him, that night and all the nights after it. Sometimes he'd smile back. But sometimes his face would be full of an intensity that couldn't be contained in a smile. Whenever Lisa saw that, her eyes would widen, her lips would part, and she'd look frightened and fascinated all at once. Which made me feel worse than if he'd smiled at her.

And sometimes he would ignore her completely, as if she were a cup of coffee he hadn't ordered. Then her face would close up tight with puzzlement and hurt, and I'd want to break something.

I could have hated him, but it was just as well I didn't. I wanted to learn music from Willy and to be near Lisa. Lisa wanted to be near Willy. The perfect arrangement. Hah.

And who could know what Willy wanted?

FOURTH OF July, Independence Day 1970, promised to be the emotional climax of the summer. Someone had organized a day of Vietnam War protests, starting with a rally in Riverside Park and ending with a torchlight march down State Street. Posters about it were everywhere—tacked to telephone poles, stuck on walls, and all over the tables at Orpheus. The picture on the posters was the photo taken that spring, when the Ohio National Guard shot four students on the Kent State campus during another protest: a dark-haired woman kneeling over a dead student's body, her head lifted, her mouth open with weeping or screaming. You'd think a photo like that would warn you away from protesting. But it gives you the feeling that someone has to do something. It gets you out on the street.

Steve was having a special marathon concert at the coffeehouse: Sherman and Henley, the Rose Hip String Band, Betsy Kaske, and—surprise—Willy Silver and John Deacon. True, we were scheduled to go on at seven, when the audience would be smallest, but I didn't care. I had been hired to play. For money.

The only cloud on my horizon was that Willy was again treating Lisa as one of life's nonessentials. As we set up for the show, I could almost see a dotted line trailing behind Willy that was her gaze, fixed on him.

Evening light was slanting through the door when we hit the stage, which made me feel funny. Orpheus was a place for after dark, when its shabby, struggling nature was cloaked with night-and-music magic. But Willy set his fiddle under his chin, leaned into the microphone, and drew out with his bow one sweet, sad, sustained note. All the awareness in the room—his, mine, and our dozen or so of audience's—hurtled to the sharp point of that one note and balanced there. I began to pick the banjo softly and his note changed, multiplied, until we were playing instrumental harmony. I sang, and if my voice broke a little, it was just what the song required:

> *"The sun rises bright in France, and fair sets he,*
> *Ah, but he has lost the look he had in my ain country."*

We made enough magic to cloak *three* shabby coffeehouses with glamour. When I got up the nerve to look beyond the edge of the stage, sometime in our fourth song, we had another dozen listeners. They'd come to line State Street for the march and our music had called them in.

Lisa sat on the shag rug in front of the stage. Her eyes were bright, and for once, her attention didn't seem to be all for Willy.

Traditional music mostly tells stories. We told a lot of them that night. I felt them all as if they'd happened to friends of mine. Willy seemed more consumed by the music than the words, and the songs he sang were sometimes almost too beautiful. But his strong voice never quavered or cracked like mine did. His guitar and fiddle were gorgeous, always, perfect and precise.

We finished at eight-thirty with a loose and lively rendition of "Blues in the Bottle," and the room was close to full. The march was due to pass by in half an hour.

We bounded offstage and into the back room. "Yo," said Willy, and stuck out his right hand. I shook it. He was touched with craziness, a little drunk with the music. He looked . . . not quite domesticated. Light seemed to catch more than usual in his green eyes. He radiated a contained energy that could have raised the roof.

"Let's go look at the street," I said.

We went out the back door and up the short flight of outside stairs to State Street. Or where State Street had been. The march, contrary to the laws of physics governing crowds, had arrived early.

Every leftist in Illinois might have been there. The pavement was gone beneath a winding, chanting snake of marchers blocks and blocks and *blocks* long. Several hundred people singing "Give Peace a Chance" makes your hair stand on end. Willy nudged me, beaming, and pointed to a banner that read DRAFT BEER, NOT BOYS.

There really were torches, though the harsh, yellow-tinted lights of State Street faded them. Some people on the edge of the crowd had lit sparklers; as the line of march passed over the bridge, first one, then dozens of sparklers, like shooting stars, arced over the railings and into the river, with one last bright burst of white reflection on the water before they hit.

I wanted to follow the march, but my banjo was in the coffeehouse, waiting for me to look after it. "I'm going to see what's up inside," I shouted at Willy. He nodded. Sparklers, fizzing, reflected in his eyes.

The crowd packed the sidewalk between me and Orpheus's front door, so I retraced our steps, down the stairs and along the river. I came into the parking lot, blind from the lights I'd just left, and heard behind me, "Hey, hippie."

There were two of them, about my age. They were probably both on their school's football and swimming teams; their hair was short, they weren't wearing blue jeans, they smelled of Southern Comfort, and they'd called me "hippie." A terrible combination. I started to walk away, across the parking lot, but the blond one stepped forward and grabbed my arm.

"Hey! I'm talking to you."

There's nothing helpful you can say at times like this, and if there had been, I was too scared to think of it. The other guy, brown haired and shorter, came up and jabbed me in the stomach with two fingers. "You a draft dodger?" he said. "Scared to fight for your country?"

"Hippies make me puke," the blond one said thoughtfully.

They were drunk, for God's sake, and out on the town, and as excited in their way by the mass of people on the street above as I was. Which didn't make me feel any better when the brown-haired one punched me in the face.

I was lying on my back clutching my nose and waiting for the next bad thing to happen to me when I heard Willy say, "Don't do it." I'd heard him use his voice in more ways than I could count, but never before like that, never a ringing command that could turn you to stone.

I opened my eyes and found my two tormenters bracketing me, the blond one's foot still raised to kick me in the stomach. He lost his balance as I watched and got the foot on the ground just in time to keep from falling over. They were both looking toward the river railing, so I did, too.

The parking lot didn't have any lights to reflect in his eyes. The green sparks there came from inside him. Nor was there any wind to lift and stir his hair like that. He stood very straight and tall, six meters from us, his hands held a little out from his sides like a gunfighter in a cowboy movie. Around his right hand, like a living glove, was a churning outline of golden fire. Bits of it dripped away like liquid from the ends of his fingers, evaporating before they hit the gravel. Like sparks from a sparkler.

I'm sure that's what my two friends told each other the next day—that he'd had a sparkler in his hand, and the liquor had made them see something more. That they'd been stupid to run away. But it wasn't a sparkler. And they weren't stupid. I heard them running across the parking lot; I watched Willy clench the fingers of his right hand and close his eyes tight, and saw the fire dim slowly and disappear. And I wished like hell that I could run away, too.

He crouched down beside me and pulled me up to sitting. "Your nose is bleeding."

"What are you?" I croaked.

The fire was still there, in his eyes. "None of your business," he said. He put his arm around me and hauled me to my feet. I'm not very heavy, but it still should have been hard work, because I didn't help. He was too slender to be so strong.

"What do you mean, none of my business? Jesus!"

He yanked me around to face him. When I looked at him, I saw wildness and temper and a fragile control over both. "I'm one of the Daoine Sidhe, Johnny-lad," he said, and his voice was harsh and colored by traces of some accent. "Does that help?"

"No," I said, but faintly. Because whatever that phrase meant, he was admitting that he was not what I was. That what I had seen had really been there.

"Try asking Steve. Or look it up, I don't care."

I shook my head. I'd forgotten my nose; a few drops of blood spattered from it and marked the front of his white shirt. I stood frozen with terror, waiting for his reaction.

It was laughter. "Earth and Air," he said when he caught his breath, "are we doing melodrama or farce out here? Come on, let's go lay you down and pack your face in ice."

There was considerable commotion when we came in the back door. Lisa got the ice and hovered over me while I told Steve about the two guys. I said Willy had chased them off; I didn't say how. Steve was outraged, and Lisa was solicitous, and it was all wasted on me. I lay on the floor with a cold nose and a brain full of rug fuzz, and let all of them do or say whatever they felt like.

Eventually I was alone in the back room, with the blank ceiling tiles to look at. Betsy Kaske was singing "Wild Women Don't Get the Blues." I roused from my self-indulgent stupor only once, when Steve passed on his way to the kitchen.

"Steve, what's a—" and I pronounced Daoine Sidhe as best I could.

He repeated it, and it sounded more like what Willy had said. "Elves," he added.

"What?"

"Yeah. It's an Irish name for the elves."

"Oh, Christ," I said. When I didn't add to that, he went on into the kitchen.

I don't know what I believed. But after a while I realized that I hadn't seen Lisa go by in a long time. And she didn't know what I knew, or almost knew. So I crawled up off the floor and went looking for her.

Not in the front room, not in the kitchen, and if she was in the milling people who were still hanging out on State Street, I'd never find her, anyway. I went out to the back steps, to see if she was in the parking lot.

Yes, sort of. They stood in the deep shadow where Orpheus's back wall joined the jutting flank of the next building. Her red-gold hair was a dim cascade of lighter color in the dark. The white streak in his was like a white bird, flying nowhere. And the pale skin of her face and arms, his pale face and white shirt, sorted out the rest of it for me. Lisa was so small and light boned, he'd lifted her off her feet entirely. No work at all for him. Her arms were around his neck. One of his hands was closed over her shoulder—I could see his long fingers against her dark blouse—and the gesture was so intense, so hungry, that it seemed as if that one hand alone could consume her. I turned and went back into Orpheus, cold, frightened, and helpless.

Lisa didn't come back until a little before closing, several hours later. I know; I was keeping watch. She darted in the back door and snatched her shoulder bag from the kitchen. Her eyes were the only color in her face: gray, rimmed with red. "Lisa!" I called.

She stopped with her back to me. "What?"

I didn't know how to start. Or finish. "It's about Willy."

"Then I don't want to hear it."

"But—"

"John, it's none of your business. And it doesn't matter now, anyway."

She shot me one miserable, intolerable look before she darted out the back door and was gone. She could look like that and tell me it was none of my business?

———

I'D HELPED Steve clean up and lock up, and pretended that I was going home. But at three in the morning I was sitting on the back steps, watching a newborn breeze ruffle a little heap of debris caught against the doorsill: a crushed paper cup, a bit of old newspaper, and one of the flyers for the march. When I looked up from it Willy was standing at the bottom of the steps.

"I thought you'd be back tonight," I said.

"Maybe that's why I came back. Because you thought it so hard." He didn't smile, but he was relaxed and cheerful. After making music with him almost every day for a month, I could tell. He dropped loose limbed onto the bottom step and stretched his legs out in front of him.

"So. Have you told her? What you are?"

He looked over his shoulder at me with a sort of stunned disbelief. "Do you mean Lisa? Of course not."

"Why not?" All my words sounded to me like little lead fishing weights hitting the water: *plunk, plunk.*

"Why should I? Either she'd believe me or she wouldn't. Either one is about equally tedious."

"Tedious."

He smiled, that wicked, charming, conspiratorial smile. "John, you can't think I care if Lisa believes in fairies."

"What *do* you care about?"

"John. . . ," he began, wary and a little irritable.

"Do you care about her?"

And for the second time, I saw it: his temper on a leash. "What the hell does it matter to you?" He leaned back on his elbows and exhaled loudly. "Oh, right. You want her for yourself. But you're too scared to do anything about it."

That hurt. I said, a little too quickly, "It matters to me that she's happy. I just want to know if she's going to be happy with you."

"No," he snapped. "And whether she's going to be happy *without* me is entirely her lookout. Rowan and Thorn, John, I'm tired of her. And if you're not careful, I'll be tired of you, too."

I looked down at his scornful face and remembered Lisa's: pale, red eyed. I described Willy Silver, aloud, with words my father had forbidden in his house.

He unfolded from the step, his eyes narrowed. "Explain to me, before I paint the back of the building with you. I've always been nice to you. Isn't that enough?" He said "nice" through his teeth.

"Why are you nice to me?"

"You're the only one who wants something important from me."

"Music?"

"Of course, music."

The rug fuzz had been blown from my head by his anger and mine. "Is that why you sing that way?"

"What the devil is wrong with the way I sing?"

"Nothing. Except you don't sound as if any of the songs ever happened to you."

"Of course they haven't." He was turning stiff and cold, withdrawing. That seemed worse than when he was threatening me.

The poster for the protest march still fluttered in the doorway. I grabbed it and held it out. "See her?" I asked, jabbing a finger at the picture of the woman kneeling over the student's body. "Maybe she knew that guy. Maybe she didn't. But she cares that he's dead. And I look at this picture, and *I* care about *her*. And all those people who marched past you in the street tonight? They did it because they care about a lot of people that they're never even going to see."

He looked fascinated and horrified at once. "Don't you all suffer enough as it is?"

"Huh?"

"Why would you take someone else's suffering on yourself?"

I didn't know how to answer that. I said finally, "We take on each other's happiness, too."

He shook his head, slowly. He was gathering the pieces of himself together, putting all his emotional armor back on. "This is too strange even for me. And among my people, I'm notoriously fond of strange things." He turned and walked away, as if I'd ceased to exist.

"What about tonight?" I said. He'd taken about a half-dozen steps. "Why did you bother to scare off those guys who were beating me up?"

He stopped. After a long moment he half turned and looked at me, wild eyed and . . . frightened? Then he went on, stiffly, across the parking lot, and disappeared into the dark.

The next night, when I came in, Willy's guitar and fiddle were gone. But Steve said he hadn't seen him.

Lisa was clearing tables at closing, her hair falling across her face and hiding it. From behind that veil, she said, "I think you should give up. He's not coming."

I jumped. "Was I that obvious?"

"Yeah." She swept the hair back and showed a wry little smile. "You looked just like me."

"I feel lousy," I told her. "I helped drive him away, I think."

She sat down next to me. "I wanted to jump off the bridge

last night. But the whole time I was saying, 'Then he'll be sorry, the rat.'"

"He wouldn't have been."

"Nope, not a bit," she said.

"But I would have."

She raised her gray cat-eyes to my face. "I'm not going to fall in love with you, John."

"I know. It's okay. I still would have been sorry if you jumped off the bridge."

"Me, too," Lisa said. "Hey, let's make a pact. We won't talk about The Rat to anybody but each other."

"Why?"

"Well . . ." She frowned at the empty, lighted space of the stage. "I don't think anybody else would understand."

So we shared each other's suffering, as he put it. And maybe that's why we wouldn't have called it that.

===

I DID see him again, though.

State Street had been gentrified, and Orpheus, the building, even the parking lot, had fallen to a downtown mall where there was no place for shabbiness or magic—any of the kinds of magic that were made that Fourth of July. These things happen in twice seven long years. But there are lots more places like that, if you care to look.

I was playing at the Greenbriar Bluegrass Festival in Pocahontas County, West Virginia. Or rather, my band was. A columnist in *Folk Roots* magazine described us so:

> Bird That Whistles drives traditional bluegrass fans crazy. They have the right instrumentation, the right licks—and they're likely to apply them to Glenn Miller's "In the Mood," or the Who's "Magic Bus." If you go to see them, leave your preconceptions at home.

I was sitting in the cookhouse tent that served as the musicians' green room, drinking coffee and watching the chaos that is thirty-some traditional musicians all tuning and talking and eating at once. Then I saw, over the heads, a raven's-wing black one with a white streak.

In a few minutes, he stood in front of me. He didn't look five minutes older than he had at Orpheus. He wasn't nervous, exactly, but he wasn't at ease, either.

"Hi," I said. "How'd you find me?"

"With this," he answered, smiling a little. He held out an article clipped from a Richmond, Virginia, paper. It was about the festival, and the photo was of Bird That Whistles.

"I'm glad you did."

He glanced down suddenly. "I wanted you to know that I've been thinking over what you told me."

I knew what he was talking about. "All this time?"

Now it was the real thing, his appealing grin. "It's a damned big subject. But I thought you'd like to know . . . well, sometimes I understand it."

"Only sometimes?"

"Rowan and Thorn, John, have mercy! I'm a slow learner."

"The hell you are. Can you stick around? You could meet the band, do some tunes."

"I wish I could," he said, and I think he meant it.

"Hey, wait a minute." I pulled a paper napkin out of the holder on the table and rummaged in my banjo case for a pen.

"What's that?" he asked, as I wrote.

"My address. I'm living in Detroit now, God help me. If you ever need anything—or even if you just want to jam—let me know, will you?" And I slid the napkin across the table to him.

He reached out, hesitated, traced the edges of the paper with one long, thin finger. "Why are you giving me this?"

I studied that bent black-and-white head, the green eyes

half veiled with his lids and following the motion of his finger. "You decide," I told him.

"All right," he said softly, "I will." If there wasn't something suspiciously like a quaver in his voice, then I've never heard one. He picked up the napkin. "I won't lose this," he said, with an odd intensity. He put out his right hand, and I shook it. Then he turned and pushed through the crowd. I saw his head at the door of the tent; then he was gone.

I stared at the top of the table for a long time, where the napkin had been, where his finger had traced. Then I took the banjo out of its case and put it into mountain minor tuning.

ROGER   ZELAZNY

Kalifriki
of the Thread

*Tops of different sorts, and jointed dolls,
and fair, golden
apples from the clear-voiced Hesperides. . . .*

ORPHEUS THE THRACIAN

THIS IS the story of Kalifriki of the Thread, the Kife, and the toymaker's daughter—in the days of the shifter's flight from the Assassin's Garden, wherefrom it bore a treasure almost without price. But even a Kife can be followed by a Master of the Thread. For the Thread may wander anywhere and need not have an end; the Thread has more sides than a sword; the Thread is subtle in its turnings, perhaps infinite in the variations it may play in the labyrinths of doom, destiny, desire. No one, however, can regard every turning of fate from the

Valley of Frozen Time. Attempts to do so tend to terminate in madness.

When the man tracked the Kife to the ice-feik and slew it there, the Kife knew it was in trouble, for it was the third time the man had reached it, the third world upon which he had found it, and the third time that he had slain it, a feat none had ever accomplished before.

Now, five times in a year is the charm for destruction of a Kife, and it seemed that this one suspected as much, for he had managed the pursuit as none had ever done before. The Kife did not understand how the man had located it and reached it, and it realized it was important that it learn as much as possible before the lights went out.

So it stared at the hunter—hammer jawed, high of cheek, dark eyed beneath an oddly sensitive brow, dark hair tied back with a strip of blue cloth. The man still held the trident which had emitted the vibrations that had shattered several of the Kife's major organs, one of the few portable weapons capable of dispatching it from the high dragon form with such ease. The man wore mittens, boots, and a heavy white garment of fur, the hood thrown back now. The midnight sun stood behind his head, and stars glittered like ice moths beside his shoulders.

"And again it is you," the Kife hissed.

The other nodded. The Kife noted a slight irregularity to the man's lower teeth, a small scar beside his right eye, a piece of red thread wrapped about his left wrist.

"What is your name?" the Kife asked him.

"I am called Kalifriki," said the man.

"How do you do what you do?"

For the first time, the man smiled.

"I might ask the same of you," he replied.

"Shifter's secret," the Kife answered.

"To all tricks their trades," said the man.

"And why you?" the Kife asked.

Kalifriki continued to smile. If he replied, the Kife did not hear it. It felt the death seize and squeeze, and as the world went away it saw the man reach to touch the Thread.

Kalifriki watched as the body collapsed, fuming, leaving him with only the green and silver-scaled hide. As the essence emerged, he reached forward and trailed the Thread through it. At that moment, it was difficult to see precisely where the strand began or ended. The man's gaze followed it into the smoky distance, and then he moved.

There is a timeless instant where the world hangs frozen before you. It is map, sculpture, painting; it is not music, words, or wind. You may survey the course of your Thread through its time and space, attempt a rapid adjustment. Then the ice of Time is broken, the flow tugs at the strand of your existence, and you are drawn into the game.

———

THE KIFE came to consciousness without breaking the rhythm of its six arms as they chipped delicately at the mineral encrustations. The sky was black above its burnished head, gem-quality stars strewn wherever it looked. Frost came and went upon its body surfaces, dialogue of thermostat and environment.

It had not had time to choose well because of the conversation preceding its departure from the other world. This shifting had almost been a shot in the dark. Almost.

But not quite. Here, there was a little mental trick, a tuning. . . .

Yes.

It could reach back into the larger brain, shielded within a distant cave, which oversaw the operation of the entire robot prospecting team. The brain operated at perhaps 10 percent of capacity. It drowsed. It almost sleepwalked its charges through their chores. But this was sufficient. The job was, in this fashion, adequately performed. If more brain work were needed, it would rise to the occasion. Only—

It infiltrated several circuits, then paused. There was no resistance. Like a rising tide, it flowed farther, ebbed, flowed, ebbed. The processor in the cave drowsed on. The Kife saw that it had long ago set alarms. So long as nothing interfered with the robot team's collection of minerals, it was content to contemplate a randomized hypothesis program it had designed, called "dreaming." Perceiving this, the Kife extended the rest of itself into the thinking space it required.

Now, now there were places beyond the routines, room to manipulate memories and ideas, to reason, to imagine at levels none of the other robots could achieve.

The Kife recalled the man who had slain it a world away. It remembered how the telepathic hunting pack, the Necrolotti, had fled from the man, having sensed a predator more dangerous than themselves. The man Kalifriki was a hunter, a killer, with the ability to traverse the side-by-side lands. It struck the Kife then that the two of them had much in common. But it did not believe that the man was of its own kind. That is, he shifted, but the means he employed bore no resemblance to the Kife's own methods.

It pondered the hunter's motives. Vengeance? For any of the numerous acts which might have gained it the hatred of someone it had underestimated? It thought then of their duel on the world before the ice-feik. No, there was no passion there. If someone wanted vengeance, it had to be some other, which, of course, would make the man a professional at the business.

Recovery? The man might be after it to obtain a thing it had taken. The Kife sought, in its hip compartment, after the item it had transformed considerable dragon-mass to energy in order to transport. Yes, it was intact. It occurred to it then that a mission of both vengeance and recovery was not out of the question. The one certainly did not preclude the other. . . .

But might it be made to? It toyed with the thought. It had died twice now because it had been surprised, and once because it had underestimated its adversary. And it had been surprised and had underestimated because so few creatures were truly a threat to Kife-kind. The Kife were rare in the side-by-side lands because of their ferocity. Each required a large range, and they kept their numbers low by means of quick, lethal, territorial disputes with each other. But beyond another Kife, there wasn't much that a Kife feared. Realistically, the Kife now added Kalifriki to the list. The man was particularly dangerous because the Kife was uncertain as to his motives or the full range of his abilities. Best to devote thought to ensuring against another surprise. But perhaps, just possibly, it should consider the terms of a bargain.

The days passed, barely distinguishable from the nights, and the Kife fell into the rock-harvesting routine. It conveyed the minerals to a truck, troubled only by the occasional seizing up of a limb. Twice, the truck's storage compartment was filled and the Kife drove it to the warehousing area where other robots unloaded it. The second time this was being done a servicing unit approached, fastened leads to sockets beneath its backplates, and performed a series of tests.

"You are due for a major overhaul," it broadcast. "We will send another to tend to your diggings and perform this servicing now."

"I am functioning fine, and I am in the midst of a complicated excavation," the Kife replied. "Do it next time."

"There is some leeway," the servicing unit admitted. "We will do it next time, as you say."

As the Kife headed back to its diggings it pondered a fresh dilemma. It could not permit itself to undergo a major servicing, for the special item it carried would be discovered and perhaps damaged during the course of it. Nor was the item the sort of thing it could merely hide for a long period of time.

The low temperatures which prevailed in this place would doubtless damage it.

Perhaps it were better simply to flee to another place. Only—

Only *this* might represent a problem. It had heard stories of shifters who could wait in the Valley of Frozen Time, watching another, waiting until that other moved to shift, and then pouncing. The Kife could not perform this feat, though it had often tried. The tale could well be apocryphal, for it had also heard that that way lay madness. Still, it were better not to underestimate the one called Kalifriki.

Therefore, it was better to remain at work. To remain, and to figure a means whereby it might manage the overhaul.

And so it slowed its pace, collecting minerals at half the rate it had earlier, saving wear and tear on its body and postponing another confrontation with a servicing unit. Still, the call took it by surprise.

"Prospector unit, are you damaged?" came the broadcast message.

"I am not," it replied.

"You have been in the field much longer than usual. Is there a problem?"

"The work goes slowly."

"Perhaps the vein has been played out and you should be relocated."

"I think not. I have just uncovered a fresh deposit."

"It has been a long while since you have been overhauled."

"I know."

"Therefore, we are sending a mobile unit to your diggings, to service you in the field."

"That will not be necessary. I will be coming in before long."

"You are beyond the safety limit. We will dispatch a mechanic unit."

The transmission ended. The Kife made a decision. It was

difficult to estimate when the service unit would arrive. But it was determined to undergo the servicing rather than flee. This required that it secrete the item. At least, it had discovered a means for preserving it outside its own body for a brief while, with the recent discovery of a cave subjected to geothermal heating by way of a deep pit in its floor.

It departed the work area, traveling to the opening in the side of a fractured ridge. Wisps of steam moved about it, and when the ground rumbled lightly these puffed more forcefully toward the heavens. It flicked on its dome light as it worked its way into the opening and entered the chamber where the pit glowed red-orange and gravel occasionally rattled across the floor. It halted at the rim, staring downward. The level of the bubbling magma seemed somewhat higher, but not so much so as to represent a danger to anything left in the chamber. Nor, according to its sensors, was there an increase in seismic activity since the time it had discovered this opening. Yes, this would be an ideal place to store it for a few hours while—

There came a flash of light from the entranceway, and its sensors read heat overload as one of its forelimbs was fused. Turning, it beheld a humanoid figure in a pressurized suit, light in one hand, pistol in the other. It also noted the strand of red wrapped around the figure's forearm.

"Kalifriki!" It broadcast on the wavelength used for general communication in this place. "Hold your fire or you may defeat your own purposes."

"Oh?" The man answered at the same frequency. "When did you become aware of my purposes?"

"You were not hired simply to destroy me, but to recover something I took, were you not?"

"Actually, I was hired to do both," Kalifriki replied.

"Then it was the Old Man of Alamut who retained you?"

"Indeed. When the Assassins need to hire an assassin they come to Kalifriki."

"Would you consider making a deal?"

"Your life for the vial? No, I'd rather collect the entire fee."

"I was not really offering. I was merely curious," said the Kife, "whether you would accept."

Kalifriki's weapon flared as the Kife charged him.

Two more of its six forearms were melted by the bright discharge, and a large block of sensors was destroyed. This meant very little to the Kife, however, for it felt it could spare considerable function and still remain superior to a human. In fact—

"It was foolish of you to follow me here," it said, as it swung a blow that missed Kalifriki but pulverized a section of the cave wall. "Another robot is even now on the way."

"No," the man replied. "I faked that call to get you to come here."

"You *chose* this place? Why?"

"I was hoping you'd have produced the vial by the time I arrived," he replied, diving to his right to avoid another charge. "Unfortunately, my entry was a trifle premature. Pity."

He fired again, taking out several more sensors and a square foot of insulation. The Kife turned with incredible speed, however, knocking the pistol upward and lunging. Kalifriki triggered the weapon in that position, threw himself to the rear and rolled, dropping his light as he did so. A section of the cave's roof collapsed, half burying the Kife, blocking the entranceway.

Kalifriki rose to his feet.

"I can take a terrific beating in this body," the Kife stated, beginning to dig itself out, "and still destroy you. Whereas the slightest damage to that suit means your end."

"True," said the man, raising the weapon and pointing it once again. "Fortunately for me, that problem is already solved."

He pulled the trigger and the weapon crackled feebly and grew still.

"Oh," said the Kife, wishing his robot features capable of a smile.

Kalifriki holstered the weapon, raised a boulder, and hurled it. It smashed against the Kife's head and rolled off to the side where it fell into the pit. The Kife increased its efforts to uncover itself, working with only two appendages, as the fourth of its arms had been damaged in the rockfall.

Kalifriki continued to hurl rubble as the Kife dug itself out. Charging the man then, the Kife reached for his throat. Its left arm slowed, emitted a grating noise, and grew still. The right arm continued toward Kalifriki, who seized it with both hands and ducked beneath it, springing to the robot's side, then again to its rear. The Kife's treads left the ground in the light gravity of the moonlet. As it was turned and tipped, it felt a push. Then it was falling, the glow rushing up toward it. Before it struck the magma it realized that it had underestimated Kalifriki again.

═══

THE KIFE regarded the Valley of Frozen Time. As always, it tried to stretch the timeless moment wherein it could consider the physical prospects and some of the sequences available to it. For reasons it did not understand, the hovering process continued. It rejoiced, in that this time it saw the means whereby it might plot and manipulate events to an extent it had never achieved before. This time, not only would it be able to lay a trap for Kalifriki, but it would create one of subtlety and refinement, by a shifter, for a shifter, worthy of a shifter in all respects.

It was able to hold back the flow until almost everything was in place.

═══

As KALIFRIKI followed the Thread through the placeless time into the timeless place, he was puzzled by its course thereafter, into the world to which he was about to follow the Kife for their final confrontation. It ran through the most unusual pattern he had ever beheld. It was too complicated a thing for him to analyze in detail before its force drew him to the level of events. Therefore, he would have to trust the instincts which had served him so well in the past, regarding the array only in gross, seeking the nexus of greatest menace and providing a lifeline of some sort. Here, he would have chuckled—though laughter, like wind or music, could not manifest in this place. He twisted the strand and whipped it, the hot, red loop following his will, racing away from him among canyons and boulevards of his latest world-to-be. He followed . . .

———

. . . SETTING FOOT upon the rocky trail which gave way immediately beneath him. He reached for the passing ledge and caught hold, only to have it, too, yield as his weight came upon it. Then, through risen dust, he beheld the long, steep slope below, with several rocky prominences near which he soon must pass. He raised his left arm to protect his face, let his body go limp, and attempted to steer the course of descent with his heels as he reflected upon the prudence of dealing with a great and distant menace while neglecting a smaller but nasty one so close at hand.

———

WHEN HE woke he found himself in a large, canopied bed, his head aching, his mouth dry. The room was dark, but daylight leaked about the edges of shutters on the far wall. He attempted to rise so as to visit the window, but the pain in his right leg told him that a bone could be broken. He cursed in Norman French, Arabic, Italian, and Greek, wiped his brow, fell to musing, and passed back to sleep.

When next he woke it was to the singing of birds and the soft sounds of another's presence in the room. Through slitted eyelids, he beheld a human-sized form advancing upon him, areas of brightness moving at its back. It halted beside the bed, and he felt a cold hand upon his brow, fingertips at the pulse in his wrist. He opened his eyes.

She was blonde and dark eyed with a small chin, her face entirely unlined, expressionless in her attention. It was difficult for him to estimate whether she was tall, short, or somewhere between, in that he was uncertain as to the height of the bed. Behind her stood a gleaming simulacrum of an ape, an upright, bronze-plated chimpanzee, perfectly formed in every detail, bearing a large, dark case in its right hand. On the floor beside it stood a huge, silver tortoise, a covered tray on its back, its head turning slowly from side to side.

Only for an instant did the metallic bodies cause a rush of apprehension, as he recalled his battle with the Kife in its robot form.

Then, "Do not be distressed," he heard her say, in a language close to one of the many he spoke. "We wish only to help you."

"It was a memory come to trouble me," he explained. "Is my leg broken?"

"Yes," she replied, uncovering it. He beheld an ornate swirl of black-and-yellow metal about his lower right leg. It seemed a work of art, such as might be displayed at the Byzantine Court. "Dr. Shong set it," she added, indicating the metal ape, who bowed.

"How long ago was this?" Kalifriki asked.

She glanced at Dr. Shong, who said, "Three days—no, three and a half," in a voice like a brassy musical instrument played low and slow.

"Thank you. How did I come to this place?"

"We found you on one of our walks," Dr. Shong said, "mixed in with the remains of a rock slide, beneath a broken trail. We brought you back here and repaired you."

"What is this place?" he asked.

"This is the home of the toymaker, Jerobee Clockman, my father," the lady told him. "I am Yolara."

The question in her eyes and voice was clear.

"I am called Kalifriki," he said.

"Are you hungry—Kalifriki?" she asked.

He nodded, licking his lips. The smell of the food had become almost unbearable. "Indeed," he replied.

Dr. Shong raised him into a seated position and propped him with pillows while Yolara uncovered the tray and brought it to the bedside. She seated herself on an adjacent chair and offered him the food.

"Still warm," he observed, tasting it.

"Thank Odas," she said, gesturing toward the tortoise. "He bears a heating element in his back."

Odas met his gaze and nodded, acknowledging his thanks with, "My pleasure," rendered in a high, reedy voice, and, "Come, Doctor," he continued, "let us leave them to organic converse—unless we may be of some further service."

Yolara shook her head slightly and the pair departed.

When he finally paused between mouthfuls, Kalifriki nodded in the direction the pair had taken. "Your father's work?" he inquired.

"Yes," she answered.

"Ingenious, and lovely. Are there more such about?"

"Yes," she answered, staring at him so steadily as to make him uncomfortable. "You will meet more of them, by and by."

"And your father?"

"He is, at the moment, ill. Else he would have overseen your awakening and welcomed you in person."

"Nothing serious, I hope."

She looked away replying, "It is difficult to know. He is a reticent man."

"What of your mother?"

"I never knew her. Father says that she ran away with a Gypsy musician when I was quite young."

"Have you brothers or sisters?"

"None."

Kalifriki continued eating.

"What were you doing in these parts?" she asked after a time. "We are fairly remote from the avenues of commerce."

"Hunting," he said.

"What sort of beast?"

"It is rare. It comes from a place very far from here."

"What does it look like?"

"Anything."

"Dangerous?"

"Very."

"How is it called?"

"Kife."

She shook her head.

"I have never heard of such a creature."

"Just as well. When do you think I might get up?"

"Whenever you possess the strength. Dr. Shong says that the device you wear should protect your leg fully—though you might want a stick, for balance."

He lowered his fork.

"Yes, I would like to try . . . soon," he said.

Shortly, she removed the tray and drew the cover higher, for he had fallen asleep.

When he woke that afternoon, however, he attempted to get up after eating. Dr. Shong rushed to assist him. While Yolara fetched a stick, the ape helped him to dress, performing neurological tests and checking his muscle tone during their frequent pauses. Dr. Shong picked away the Thread that clung to Kalifriki's wrist and tossed it aside. He did not see it drift back several moments later, settling upon his own shoulder, depending toward his hip.

They were halfway across the room when Yolara returned with the stick. Both accompanied him outside then and along the corridor to a balcony, whence he looked down upon a courtyard containing six sheep, two goats, four cows, a bull, and a flock of chickens, all fashioned of metals both dull and gleaming, all seeming to browse and forage, all producing peculiar approximations of the sounds made by their flesh-and-blood models.

"Amazing," Kalifriki stated.

"They are merely decorative machines, not possessed of true intellect," Dr. Shong observed. "They are but child's play for the Master."

"Amazing, nevertheless," said Kalifriki.

Yolara took his arm to steady him as he turned away, heading back inside.

"We'll return you to your room now," she said.

"No," he replied, turning toward a stairwell they had passed on their way up the hall. "I must go farther."

"Not stairs. Not yet," said Dr. Shong.

"Please do as he says," she asked. "Perhaps tomorrow."

"Only if we may walk to the far end of the hallway and back."

She glanced at the metal simian, who nodded.

"Very well. But let us go slowly. Why must you push yourself so hard?"

"I must be ready to face the Kife, anywhere, anytime."

"I doubt you will find it lurking hereabouts."

"Who knows?" he replied.

That evening, Kalifriki was awakened by strains of a wild music, faint in the distance. After a time, he struggled to his feet and out into the corridor. The sounds were coming up from the stairwell. Leaning against the wall, he listened for a long while, then limped back to bed.

The following day, after breakfast, he expressed his desire for a longer walk, and Yolara dismissed Dr. Shong and led Kalifriki down the stairs. Only gradually did he come to understand the enormous size of the building through which they moved.

"Yes," she commented when he remarked upon this. "It is

built upon the ruins of an ancient abbey, and over the years it has served as fortress as well as residence."

"Fascinating," he said. "Tell me, I thought that I heard music last night. Was there some sort of celebration?"

"You might call it that," she answered. "My father left his rooms for the first time in a long while, and he summoned his musicians to play for him."

"I am glad that he is feeling better," Kalifriki said. "It was an eerie and beautiful music. I would like to hear it again one day—and perhaps even be present when the musicians perform it."

"They are returned to their crypts, somewhere beneath the floor," she said. "But who knows?"

"They, too, are creations of your father?"

"I think so," she answered. "But I've never really seen them, so it is difficult to say."

They passed an aviary of bronze birds, peculiar blue patina upon their wings, warbling, trilling, crying *kerrew* and fanning their feathers like turquoise screens. Some of them sat upon iron perches, some on nests of copper. A few of the nests contained silver eggs, while some held tiny birds, unfledged, beaks open to receive flies of foil, worms of tin. The air blurred and flashed about the singers when they moved.

In a garden in a southern courtyard she showed him a silver tree, bearing gleaming replicas of every sort of fruit he had ever seen and many he had not.

Passing up a corridor, Yolara halted before what Kalifriki at first took to be a portrait of herself, wearing a low-cut gown of black satin, a large emerald pendant in the shape of a ship riding the swells of her breasts. But upon closer regard the woman seemed more mature—

"My mother," Yolara said.

"Lovely," Kalifriki replied, "also."

At the end of the corridor was a red metal top as large as himself, spinning with a sad note, balanced upon the point of a dagger. Yolara told him that the top would rotate for ninety-nine years undisturbed.

She stated this so seriously that Kalifriki chuckled.

"I have not heard you laugh nor seen you smile," he said, "the entire time I've been here."

"These things are not fresh to me as they are to you," she replied. "I see them every day."

He nodded.

"Of course," he said.

Then she smiled. She squeezed his hand with a surprisingly firm grip.

The following day they went riding great horned horses of metal—he, mounted upon a purple stallion; she, a green mare. They sat for a long while on a hilltop, regarding the valley, the mountains, and the fortress of Jerobee Clockman. He told her somewhat of himself and her fascination seemed genuine, well beyond the point of courtesy. She seemed awkward when he finally kissed her, and it was not until the slow ride back that she told him she knew no humans other than her father, having met only an occasional merchant, minstrel, or messenger for brief spans of time.

"That seems a very odd way to live," he commented.

"Really?" she replied. "I was beginning to suspect this from reading books in the library. But since they are fiction to begin with, I could never be certain what parts are real."

"Your father seems a peculiar man," said Kalifriki. "I would like to meet him."

"I am not sure he is entirely recovered," she said. "He has been avoiding me somewhat." Riding farther, she added, "I *would* like to see more of the world than this place."

That night when Kalifriki heard the music again he made his way slowly and quietly down the stairs. He paused just outside the hall from which the skirls and wailings flowed. Carefully, then, he lowered himself to his belly and inched forward, so that he could peer around the corner of the entranceway, his eyes but a few centimeters above the floor.

He beheld a metallic quartet with the blasted forms and visages of fallen angels. They were all of them crippled, their gray, gold, and silver bodies scorched, faces pocked, brows antlered or simply horned. Broken bat wings hung like black gossamer from their shoulders. There were two fiddlers, one piper, and one who performed on a rack of crystal bells. The music was stirring, chaotic, mesmerizing, yet somehow cold as a north wind on a winter's night. It was hardly human music, and Kalifriki found himself wondering whether the metal demons composed their own tunes. Behind them, in the floor, were five grave-sized openings, the four surrounding the fifth. Seated before them in a large, dark leather chair was a white-haired fat man whose features Kalifriki could not see, for the man had steepled his fingers and held them before his face. This did, however, draw his attention to a large sapphire ring upon the man's right hand.

When the piece was ended the creatures grew still. The man rose to his feet and took hold of a slim, red lance leaning against the nearest wall. Taking several steps forward, he struck its butt upon a crescent-shaped flagstone. Immediately, the musicians swiveled in place, approached their crypts, and descended into them. When they were below the level of the floor, stone covers slid into place, concealing all traces of their existence.

The man placed the lance upon a pair of pegs on the wall to his left, then crossed the room and went out of a door at its far end. Cautiously, Kalifriki rose, entered, and moved through. At the far door, he saw the form of the man reach the end of a hallway and begin mounting a stair, which he knew from an earlier walk to lead to the building's highest tower. He waited for a long while before taking down the lance. When he struck its butt against the curved stone, the floor opened and he stared down into the crypts.

The demon musicians emerged and stood, raising their instruments, preparing to play. But Kalifriki had already seen all that he cared to. He struck the stone once more and the quartet retired again. He restored the lance to its pegs and departed the hall.

For a long time he wandered the dim corridors, lost in thought. When, at length, he passed a lighted room and saw it to be a library with Dr. Shong seated within, reading, he paused.

"Kalifriki," said the doctor, "what is the matter?"

"I think better when I pace."

"You are still recovering and sleep will serve you more than thought."

"That is not how I am built. When I am troubled I pace and think."

"I was not aware of this engineering peculiarity. Tell me your trouble and perhaps I can help you."

"I have not yet met my host. Is Jerobee Clockman aware of my presence here?"

"Yes. I report to him every day."

"Oh. Has he any special orders concerning me?"

"To treat your injury, to feed you, and to see that you are extended every courtesy."

"Has he no desire to meet me in person?"

The doctor nodded.

"Yes, but I must remind you that he has not been well himself of late. He is sufficiently improved now, however, that he will be inviting you to dine with him tomorrow."

"Is it true that Yolara's mother ran off with a musician?" Kalifriki asked.

"So I have heard. I was not present in those days. I was created after Yolara was grown."

"Thank you, Doctor," Kalifriki said, "and good night."

He limped on up to the hallway. When he turned the corner the limp vanished. Farther along the corridor he seated himself upon a bench, rolled up his trouser leg, and removed the elaborate brace he wore. Slowly, he rose to his feet. Then he shifted his weight. Then he smiled.

===

LATER THAT evening Yolara heard a scratching upon her door.

"Who is it?" she asked.

"Kalifriki. I want to talk to you."

"A moment," she said.

She opened the door. He noted she was still fully clothed in the garments she had worn that day.

"How did you know which door was mine?" she asked him.

"I stepped outside and looked up," he replied. "This was the only room with a light on—apart from mine and the library, where I left Dr. Shong. And I know your father's rooms are in the North Tower."

She granted him her second smile.

"Ingenious," she stated. "What is it you wish to talk about?"

"First, a question—if I may."

"Surely." She stepped aside and held the door wide. "Please come in."

"Thank you."

He took the chair she offered him, then said, "When I awoke several days ago, Dr. Shong told me that I had been found at the scene of my accident three and a half days earlier."

She nodded.

"Were you present when I was discovered?"

"No," she answered. "I heard of you later."

"He used the pronoun 'we,' so I assumed that you were included. Do you know who else was with him?"

She shook her head.

"One of the other simulacra, most likely," she said. "But it might also have been my father. I think not, though, because of his illness."

"Yolara," he said, "something is wrong in this place. I feel that we are both in great danger. You have said that you would like to leave. Very well. Get some things together and I'll take you away, right now, tonight."

Her eyes widened.

"This is so abrupt! I would have to tell my father! I—"

"No!" he said. "He is the one I fear. I believe he is mad, Yolara—and very dangerous."

"He would never harm me," she said.

"I would not be too certain. You resemble your mother strongly, if that portrait be true. In his madness he may one day confuse you with her memory. Then you would be in danger."

Her eyes narrowed.

"You must tell me why you say this."

"I believe that he found your mother after her affair with the Gypsy, and that he killed her."

"How can you say that?"

"I've been to the hall where he keeps his demon quartet. I have opened their crypts—and a fifth one about which they assemble to play. In that fifth one is a skeleton. About its neck is the chain bearing the emerald ship which she is wearing in the painting."

"No! I do not believe it!"

"I am sorry."

"I must see this for myself."

"I would rather you did not."

"To make a charge like that and ask me to accept it on faith is too much," she stated. "Come! It would not be as bad as you may think, for my mother is a stranger to me. I would see this crypt."

"Very well."

He rose to his feet and they passed outside. Reaching into a shadowy alcove, he produced a length of bright steel, which he kept in his right hand as he led the way to the stairs.

"Where did you get the sword?" she asked.

"Borrowed it from a suit of armor downstairs."

"My father is a sick old man. It is hardly necessary to arm yourself against him."

"Then no harm is done," he replied.

"There is even more to this," she said, "isn't there?"

"We shall see," he answered.

When they came to the hall he had visited earlier, Kalifriki took the red lance down from the wall.

"Stand here," he directed, leading her to a place near to the middle crypt, and he stepped back and smote the crescent stone with the lance's butt.

The stones slid back and he hurried to her side. Her scream was not caused by the demons which rose to surround them, however. Looking down into the crypt, Kalifriki beheld the body of a fat, white-haired man whose head had been twisted around so that it faced completely to the rear. The body lay in the embrace of the ancient skeleton from whose neck the emerald ship depended.

"Who did this?" she asked.

"I don't know," Kalifriki said. "He was not there earlier. I don't understand. I—"

He knelt suddenly and reached down into the crypt. He raised the man's right hand.

"What is it?" she asked.

"A ring with a blue stone in it," he said. "He was wearing it earlier this evening. Now he is not."

"His signet," she said. "His seal as Master Toymaker. He would never part with it willingly."

Just then the demon quartet began to play and words became impossible. Lowering the toymaker's hand, Kalifriki picked up the red lance, which he had laid aside. He rose to his feet.

He passed between the crippled demons, and when he came to the crescent stone he struck it with the lance. Immediately, the music died. The performers retired to their crypts. The crypts began to close.

"Now do you at least believe that there is danger?" he said.

"Yes," she replied. "But—"

"Indeed there is," said the fat, white-haired man who entered through the far doorway, a flash of blue upon his right hand. "I heard your scream."

"Father's simulacrum," she said. "He'd often considered making one. I didn't know that he had. It's killed him and taken his place!"

The fat man smiled and advanced.

"Excellent," he said. "Hard to put one over on you, isn't it?"

"Where's its weakest spot?" Kalifriki asked her, raising the blade.

"Slightly below the navel," she answered, and he lowered the point of the weapon.

"Really," the simulacrum said, "beneath this guise of flesh you will find that you face metal against metal. It would take a good arm and a good blade to puncture me."

Kalifriki smiled.

"Shall we find out?" he asked.

The simulacrum halted.

"No, let's not," it replied. "It seems an awful waste of talent."

Its gaze moved past them then. Kalifriki turned his head, to see Dr. Shong enter through the other door.

"Doctor!" Yolara cried. "He's killed Father and taken his place!"

"I know," the ape replied, and she stared as he grinned. "He had an offer he couldn't refuse."

"My leg," Kalifriki said, "is not broken. I believe that it was, but it is healed now. That would have taken considerably longer than the few days you said it had been. I think I've been here for several weeks, that you've kept me drugged—"

"Very astute," Dr. Shong observed. "Also, correct. We had a special request of the late Jerobee Clockman. He did not finish the final adjustments until only a little while ago."

"And then you killed him!" Yolara cried.

"Just so," said the simian, nodding, "though his simulacrum did the actual physical business. But it is lèse-majesté to call us killers in the presence of assassin royalty such as your guest. Isn't that right, Kalifriki?"

"Come closer, ape," he said.

"No. You seem to have figured out everything but why. So take the final step and tell me: What was Clockman's last creation—the thing he assembled that long while you slept?"

"I . . . I don't know," Kalifriki said.

"Come in!" Dr. Shong called out.

Kalifriki watched as his own double entered the room, a sword in its hand.

"Built according to your specifications," the ape stated. "Considerably stronger, though."

"I thought the Kife had fled."

His doppelgänger bowed.

"You were incorrect," it told him.

Kalifriki slammed the butt of the lance against the crescent stone, Yolara cried, "Killer!" and rushed toward the portly simulacrum, while the doppelgänger advanced upon Kalifriki, the point of its blade describing a small circle in the air.

"By all means, let us dance," said his double, smiling, as the musicians took up their instruments and tuned them. The ape laughed, and Yolara cried out as she was thrown across the room to strike her head upon the hearthstone.

Snarling, Kalifriki turned away from his advancing double and, with a quick leap and an even quicker lunge, drove his blade into the simulacrum of Jerobee Clockman with such force that its point passed through its abdomen and protruded from its lower back. The weapon was wrenched from Kalifriki's grip as the figure suddenly raised both arms to shoulder height, extending them out to the sides, twisted its head into a bizarre position, and began the execution of a series of dance steps. With this, a small ratcheting noise commenced in the vicinity of its midsection.

Turning then, swinging the red lance in a circle, Kalifriki succeeded in parrying his double's attack. Retreating, the music swirling wildly about him, he ventured a glance at Yolara, discovering that she still had not moved. The glance almost cost him an ear, but he parried the thrust and riposted with a double-handed blow of the lance, which would have cracked a human's ribs but only slowed the simulacrum for a moment. During that movement, however, he struck it between the eyes with the butt of the weapon and, reversing it with a spin, jabbed for the abdomen with the lance's point. The attack was parried, though; and seeming to shake off all its effects, his doppelgänger pressed him again. In the distance, he heard Dr. Shong chuckle.

Then he began to retreat once again, turning, passing behind the simulacrum of Jerobee Clockman—which was now dancing in extreme slow motion and emitting periodic clanging sounds. As it shifted its weight from left foot to right, he kicked it hard and it toppled in that direction, falling directly in the path of the double. Laughing, the doppelgänger leaped over the twitching figure to continue its attack.

Kalifriki passed among the musicians then, dodging the fiddlers' bows, sidestepping to avoid collision with the bell rack. And his double came on, stamping, thrusting, parrying, and riposting. When he reached the position toward which he had been headed, Kalifriki pretended to stumble.

Predictably, the other attacked. Continuing his drop onto one knee and turning his body, Kalifriki executed a downward, rowing stroke with the lance, which caught the simulacrum behind the knees, sweeping it off balance. Springing to his feet then, Kalifriki struck it between the shoulder blades and rushed away as it toppled into the opened crypt.

Slamming the butt of the lance against the crescent stone

silenced the musicians immediately, and they tucked away their instruments, retreating toward their own crypts. Rushing among them, Kalifriki raised the lance once more to club down his doppelgänger, should it try to emerge before the crypt sealed itself. It looked up and met his gaze.

"Fool!" it cried. "You guard me while the Kife flees!"

"Dr. Shong?" Kalifriki exclaimed, suddenly knowing it to be true.

Whirling, he hurled the lance at the running ape form, just as the crypt's lid slid shut above the simulacrum. The red shaft struck the hurrying figure's left shoulder with a terrific clang as it was about to cross the threshold of the nearer door. The impact turned it completely around. Miraculously, the ape did not fall, but teetered a moment, regained its balance, then rushed across the room toward the fireplace, left arm hanging useless.

Arriving before Kalifriki could take more than three paces, Dr. Shong knelt and reached, right hand fastening about Yolara's throat.

"Stop!" cried the ape. "I can decapitate her with a single movement! And I will if you come any nearer!"

Kalifriki halted, regarding the smear of blood on her temple.

"There was a time when I thought *she* might be a simulacrum," he said.

"I had toyed with the notion," said the other, "of replacing her with a version designed to kill you after you'd fallen in love with it. But I lack sufficient knowledge of human emotions. I was afraid it might take too long, or that it might not happen. Still, it would have been a delightful way of managing it."

Kalifriki nodded.

"What now?" he asked. "We seem stalemated here. Except that she does not appear to be breathing. If this is true, your threat is meaningless."

He began to take another step.

"Stop!" The Kife rose slowly, clasping her to its breast with forearm and elbow, its hand still at her throat. "I say she still lives. If you wish to gamble with her life, come ahead."

Kalifriki paused, his eyes narrowing. In the dim light, he saw the Thread upon the shoulder and waist of the simulacrum. Slowly, he raised his left arm. The Thread was also wrapped about his wrist. It extended back over his left shoulder. It extended forward. It joined with that segment of itself which hung upon the metal ape. It passed beyond, out of the door of the room. As Kalifriki flexed his fingers, it grew taut. As he continued the movement, the Kife turned its head, bewildered, as if looking for something in several directions. When Kalifriki closed his hand into a fist, the segments of Thread which had been looped about the Kife vanished from sight, slicing their ways into the metal body.

Moments later, the simulacrum collapsed, falling to the floor in three pieces. It had been decapitated and the torso separated from the legs at the waist. Yolara lay sprawled across its midsection, and its head rolled toward Kalifriki.

As Kalifriki stepped past it, it addressed him: "I lied. She is not breathing."

Kalifriki halted, picked up the head, and drew back his arm to hurl it against the nearest wall.

"But she may breathe again," it said, lips twisting into a smile, "if you but use your head."

"What do you mean?" Kalifriki asked. "Talk!"

"That which I stole from the Old Man of the Mountain—the Elixir of Life—it would revive her."

"Where is it?"

"I will tell you, in return for your promise that you will not destroy me."

Kalifriki turned the face away from his so that the Kife would not see him smile.

"Very well," he answered. "You have my word. Where is it?"

"Hidden among the gold and silver fruit in the bowl on the table beside the far door."

Kalifriki crossed the room, searched the bowl.

"Yes," he said at last, removing the small vial.

He unstoppered it and sniffed it. He placed his finger over the bottle's mouth, inverted it, returned it to an upright position. He placed upon his tongue the single droplet which clung to his fingertip.

"It is odorless and tasteless," he observed, "and I feel nothing. Are you certain this is not some trick?"

"Do not waste it, fool! It takes only a drop!"

"Very well. You had better be telling the truth."

He returned to Yolara's side and drew downward upon her chin to open her mouth. Then he removed another drop from the vial and placed it upon her tongue.

Moments later she drew a deep breath and sighed. Shortly thereafter, her eyelids fluttered and opened.

"What," she asked him, "has happened?"

"It is over," he said, raising her and holding her. "We live, and my job is finished."

"What was your job?" she inquired.

"To recover this vial," he explained, "and to bring back the head of its thief."

The brazen ape-head began to wail.

"You have tricked me!" it cried.

"You have tricked yourself," he replied, stoppering the bottle and pocketing it, helping Yolara to her feet.

"You are in charge here now," he told her. "If the memories are too bad for you, come with me and I will try to give you some better ones."

———

Now, AS he led her through the Valley of Frozen Time, Kalifriki halted in a place that was sculpture, painting, map. He squeezed Yolara's arm and gestured at the incredible prospect which lay before them.

She smiled and nodded, just as the head of the Kife, which Kalifriki bore in his left hand, opened its mouth and bit him. He would have cursed, save that this was not a place of words (nor music, nor wind). He dropped the head, which rolled away, and he raised his hand to his mouth. The Kife's head fell into a crevice, where it rolled a considerable distance before coming to rest in precarious balance at the top of another incline, its position masked in darkest shadow. Search though he did, Kalifriki never found it, and had to settle for only half his pay, for the Old Man of Alamut is a harsh taskmaster. Still, this was not an inconsiderable amount, and with it he took Yolara on an amazing odyssey, to Byzantium, Venice, Cathay—but that is another story. The while, the Kife went mad of contemplating the turnings of fate; its brazen head fell from the ledge where it opened its jaw to scream, though this was not a place of screaming (nor music, nor wind); and it rolled the side-beside slopes down to a lane near Oxford, where a Franciscan named Roger Bacon found it. That, too, is another story. The Thread is always arriving and departing. It may wander anywhere and need not have an end.

Turntables of the Night

LOOK, CONSTABLE, what I don't understand is, surely *he* wouldn't be into blues? Because that was Wayne's life for you. A blues single. I mean, if people were music, Wayne would be like one of those scratchy old numbers, you know, rerecorded about a hundred times from the original phonograph cylinder or whatever, with some old guy with a name like Deaf Orange Robinson standing knee-deep in the Mississippi and moaning through his nose.

You'd think *he'd* be more into heavy metal or Meat Loaf or someone. But I suppose he's into everyone. Eventually.

What? Yeah. That's my van, with HELLFIRE DISCO painted on it. Wayne can't drive, you see. He's just not interested in anything like that. I remember when I got my first car and we went on holiday, and I did the driving and, okay, also the repairing, and Wayne worked the radio, trying to keep the pirate stations tuned in. He didn't really care where we went as long as it was on high ground and he could get Caroline or London or whatever. I didn't care where we went so long as we went.

I was always more into cars than music. Until now, I think. I don't think I want to drive a car again. I'd keep wondering who'd suddenly turn up in the passenger seat. . . .

Sorry. So. Yeah. The disco. Well, the deal was that I supplied the van, we split the cost of the gear, and Wayne supplied the records. It was really my idea. I mean, it seemed a pretty good bet. Wayne lives with his mum but they're down to two rooms now because of his record collection. Lots of people collect records, but I reckon Wayne really wants— wanted—to own every one that was ever made. His idea of a fun outing was going to some old store in some old town and rummaging through the stock and coming out with something by someone with a name like Sid Sputnik and the Spacemen, but the thing was, the funny thing was, you'd get back to his room and he'd go to a shelf and push all the records aside and there'd be this neat brown envelope with the name and date on it and everything—waiting.

Or he'd get me to drive him all the way to Preston or somewhere to find some guy who's a self-employed plumber now but maybe back in 1961 called himself Ronnie Sequin and made it to number 152 in the charts, just to see if he'd got a spare copy of his one record, which was really so naff you couldn't even find it in the specialist stores.

Wayne was the kind of collector who couldn't bear a hole in his collection. It was almost religious, really. He could out-talk John Peel in any case, but the records he really knew about were the ones he hadn't got. He'd wait years to get some practically demo disc from a punk group who probably died of safety-pin tetanus, but by the time he got his hands on it he'd be able to recite everything down to the name of the cleaning lady who scrubbed out the studio afterward. Like I said, a collector.

So I thought, what more do you need to run a disco?

Well, basically just about everything which Wayne hadn't got—looks, clothes, common sense, some kind of idea about electric wiring, and the ability to rabbit on like a prat. But at the time we didn't look at it like that, so I flogged the Capri and bought the van and got it nearly professionally resprayed. You can only see the words MIDLAND ELECTRICITY BOARD on it if you know where to look. I wanted it to look like the van in the "A-Team," except where theirs can jump four cars and still hare off down the road, mine has trouble with drain covers.

Yes, I've talked to the other officer about the tax and insurance and MOT. Sorry, Sergeant. Don't worry about it, I won't be driving a car ever again. Never.

We bought a load of amplifiers and stuff off Ian Curtis over in Wyrecliff because he was getting married and Tracey wanted him at home of a night, bunged some cards in newsagents' windows, and waited.

Well, people didn't exactly fall over themselves to give us gigs on account of people not really catching on to Wayne's style. You don't have to be a verbal genius to be a jock, people just expect you to say, "Hey!" and "Wow!" and "Get down and boogie" and stuff. It doesn't actually matter if you sound like a pillock, it helps them feel superior. What they don't want, when they're all getting drunk after the wedding or whatever, is for someone to stand there with his eyes flashing worse than the lights, saying things like, "There's a rather interesting story attached to this record."

Funny thing, though, is that after a while we started to get popular in a weird word-of-mouth kind of way. What started it, I reckon, was my sister Beryl's wedding anniversary. She's older than me, you understand. It turned out that Wayne had brought along just about every record ever pressed for about a year before they got married. Not just the top ten, either. The guests were all around the same age and pretty soon the room was so full of nostalgia you could hardly move. Wayne just hot-wired all their ignitions and took them for a joyride down Memory Motorway.

After that we started getting dates from what you might call the more older types, you know, not exactly kids but bits haven't started falling off yet. We were a sort of specialty disco. At the breaks people would come up to him to chat about this great number they recalled from way back or whenever and it would turn out that Wayne would always have it in the van. If they'd heard of it, he'd have it. Chances are he'd have it even if they hadn't heard of it. Because you could say this about Wayne, he was a true collector—he didn't worry whether the stuff was actually good or not. It just had to exist.

He didn't put it like that, of course. He'd say there was always something unique about every record. You might think that this is a lot of crap, but here was a man who'd gotten just about everything ever made over the last forty years and he really believed there was something special about each one. He loved them. He sat up there all through the night, in his room lined with brown envelopes, and played them one by one. Records that had been forgotten even by the people who made them. I'll swear he loved them all.

Yes, all right. But you've got to know about him to understand what happened next.

We were booked for this Halloween dance. You could tell it was Halloween because of all the little bastards running around the streets shouting, "Trickle treat," and threatening you with milk bottles.

He'd sorted out lots of "Monster Mash" type records. He looked pretty awful, but I didn't think much of it at the time. I mean, he always looked awful. It was his normal look. It came from spending years indoors listening to records, plus he had this bad heart and asthma and everything.

The dance was at . . . okay, you know all that. A Halloween dance to raise money for a church hall. Wayne said that was a big joke, but he didn't say why. I expect it was some clever reason. He was always good at that sort of thing, you know, knowing little details that other people didn't know; it used to get him hit a lot at school, except when I was around. He was the kind of skinny boy who had his glasses held together with Elastoplast. I don't think I ever saw him raise a finger to anybody, only that time when Greebo Greaves broke a record Wayne had brought to some school disco and four of us had to pull Wayne off him and pry the iron bar out of his fingers and there was the police and an ambulance and everything.

Anyway.

I let Wayne set everything up, which was one big mistake but he wanted to do it, and I went and sat down by what they called the bar, i.e., a couple of trestle tables with a cloth on it.

No, I didn't drink anything. Well, maybe one cup of the punch, and that was all fruit juice. All right, two cups.

But I know what I heard, and I'm absolutely certain about what I saw.

I think.

You get the same old bunch at these kinds of gigs. There's the organizer, and a few members of the committee, some lads from the village after the pubs shut, and maybe a few dozen other people who'd sort of drifted in because there wasn't much on the box except snooker. Everyone wore a mask but hadn't made an effort with the rest of the clothes, so it looked as though Frankenstein and Co. had all gone shopping in Marks and Sparks. There were Scouts' posters on the wall and those special kind of village hall radiators that suck the heat *in*. It smelled of tennis shoes. Just to sort of set the seal on it as one of the hot spots of the world, there was a little mirror ball spinning up the rafters. Half the little mirrors had fallen off.

All right, maybe three cups. But it had bits of apple floating in it. Nothing serious has bits of apple floating in it.

Wayne started with a few hot numbers to get them stomping. I'm speaking metaphorically here, you understand. None of this boogie-on-down stuff; all you could hear was people not being as young as they used to be.

Now, I've already said Wayne wasn't exactly cut out for the business, and that night—last night—he was worse than usual. He kept mumbling, and staring at the dancers. He mixed the records up. He even scratched one. Accidentally, I mean—the only time I've ever seen Wayne really angry, apart from the Greebo business, was when scratch music came in.

It would have been very bad manners to cut in, so at the first break I went up to him, and, let me tell you, he was sweating so much it was dropping onto the mixer.

"It's that bloke on the floor," he said, "the one in the flares."

"Methuselah?" I said.

"Don't muck about. The black silk suit with the rhinestones. He's been doing John Revolta impersonations all night. Come on, you must have noticed. Platform soles. Got a silver medallion as big as a plate. Skull mask. He was over by the door."

I hadn't seen anyone like that. Well, you'd remember, wouldn't you?

Wayne's face was frozen with fear. "You must have!"

"So what, anyway?"

"He keeps staring at me!"

I patted his arm. "Impressed by your technique, old son," I said.

I took a look around the hall. Most people were milling around the punch now, the rascals. Wayne grabbed my arm.

"Don't go away!"

"I was just going out for some fresh air."

"Don't . . ." He pulled himself together. "Don't go. Hang around. Please."

"What's up with you?"

"Please, John! He keeps looking at me in a funny way!"

He looked really frightened. I gave in. "Okay. But point him out next time."

I let him get on with things while I tried to neaten up the towering mess of plugs and adapters that was Wayne's usual contribution to electrical safety. If you've got the kind of gear we've got—okay, *had*—you can spend hours working on it. I mean, do you know how many different kinds of connectors . . . all right.

In the middle of the next number Wayne hauled me back to the decks.

"There! See him? Right in the middle!"

Well, there wasn't. There were a couple of girls dancing with each other, and everyone else were just couples who were trying to pretend the seventies hadn't happened. Any rhinestone cowboys in that lot would have stood out like a strawberry in an Irish stew. I could see that some tact and diplomacy were called for at this point.

"Wayne," I said, "I reckon you're several coupons short of a toaster."

"You can't see him, can you?"

Well, no. But . . .

. . . since he mentioned it . . .

. . . I could see the space.

There was this patch of floor around the middle of the hall, which everyone was keeping clear of. Except that they weren't avoiding it, you see, they just didn't happen to be moving into it. It was just sort of accidentally there. And it stayed there. It moved around a bit, but it never disappeared.

All right, I know a patch of floor can't move around. Just take my word for it, this one did.

The record was ending, but Wayne was still in control enough to have another one spinning. He faded it up, a bit of an oldie that they'd all know.

"Is it still there?" he said, staring down at the desk.

"It's a bit closer," I said. "Perhaps it's after a spot prize."

. . . I wanna live forever . . .

"That's right, be a great help."

. . . people will see me and cry . . .

There were quite a few more people down there now, but the empty patch was still moving around, all right, was being avoided, among the dancers.

I went and stood in it.

It was cold. It said: GOOD EVENING.

The voice came from all around me, and everything seemed to slow down. The dancers were just statues in a kind of black fog, the music a low rumble.

"Where are you?"

BEHIND YOU.

Now, at a time like this the impulse is to turn around, but you'd be amazed at how good I was at resisting it.

"You've been frightening my friend," I said.

I DID NOT INTEND TO.

"Push off."

THAT DOESN'T WORK, I AM AFRAID.

I did turn around then. He was about seven feet tall in his, yes, his platform soles. And, yes, he wore flares, but somehow you'd expect that. Wayne had said they were black, but that wasn't true. They weren't any color at all; they were simply clothes-shaped holes into Somewhere Else. Black would have looked blinding white by comparison. He did look a bit like John Travolta from the waist down, but only if you buried John Travolta for about three months.

It really was a skull mask. You could see the string.

"Come here often, do you?"

I AM ALWAYS AROUND.

"Can't say I've noticed you." And I would have done. You don't meet many seven-foot, seven-stone people every day, especially ones that walked as though they had to think about every muscle movement in advance and acted as though they were alive and dead at the same time, like Cliff Richard.

YOUR FRIEND HAS AN INTERESTING CHOICE OF MUSIC.

"Yes. He's a collector, you know."

I KNOW. COULD YOU PLEASE INTRODUCE ME TO HIM?

"Could I stop you?"

I DOUBT IT.

All right, perhaps four cups. But the lady serving said there was hardly anything in it at all except orange squash and homemade wine, and she looked a dear old soul. Apart from the Wolfman mask, that is.

But I know all the dancers were standing like statues and the music was just a faint buzz and there were these, all these blue and purple shadows around everything. I mean, drink doesn't do that.

Wayne wasn't affected. He stood with his mouth open, watching us.

"Wayne," I said, "this is—"

A FRIEND.

"Whose?" I said, and you could tell I didn't take to the person, because his flares were *huge* and he wore one of those silver identity bracelets on his wrist, the sort you could moor a battleship with, and they look so posey; the fact that his wrist was solid bone wasn't doing anything to help, either. I kept thinking there was a conclusion I ought to be jumping to, but I couldn't quite get a running start. My head seemed to be full of wool.

EVERYONE'S, he said, SOONER OR LATER. I UNDERSTAND YOU'RE SOMETHING OF A COLLECTOR.

"Well, in a small—" said Wayne.

I GATHER YOU'RE ALMOST AS KEEN AS I AM, WAYNE.

Wayne's face lit up. That was Wayne, all right. I'll swear if you shot him he'd come alive again if it meant a chance to talk about his hobby, sorry, his lifetime's work.

"Gosh," he said. "Are you a collector?"

ABSOLUTELY.

Wayne peered at him. "We haven't met before, have we?" he said. "I go to most of the collectors' meetings. Were you at the Blenheim Record Fest and Auction?"

I DON'T RECALL. I GO TO SO MANY THINGS.

"That was the one where the auctioneer had a heart attack."

OH. YES. I SEEM TO REMEMBER POPPING IN, JUST FOR A FEW MINUTES.

"Very few bargains there, I thought."

OH. I DON'T KNOW. HE WAS ONLY FORTY-THREE.

All right, Inspector. Maybe six drinks. Or maybe it wasn't the drinks at all. But sometimes you get the feeling, don't you, that you can see a little way into the future? Oh, you don't. Well, anyway. I might not have been entirely in my right mind but I was beginning to feel pretty uncomfortable about all this. Well, anyone would. Even you.

"Wayne," I said. "Stop right now. If you concentrate, he'll go away. Settle down a bit. Please. Take a deep breath. This is all wrong."

The brick wall on the other side of me paid more attention. I know Wayne when he meets fellow collectors. They have these weekend rallies. You see them in shops. Strange people. But none of them as strange as this one. He was *dead* strange.

"Wayne!"

They both ignored me. And inside my mind, bits of my brain were jumping up and down, shouting and pointing, and I couldn't let myself believe what they were saying.

OH, I'VE GOT THEM ALL, he said, turning back to Wayne. ELVIS PRESLEY, BUDDY HOLLY, JIM MORRISON, JIMI HENDRIX, JOHN LENNON. . . .

"Fairly wide spread, musically," said Wayne. "Have you got the complete Beatles?"

NOT YET.

And I swear they started to talk records. I remember Mr. Friend saying he'd got the complete seventeenth-, eighteenth-, and nineteenth-century composers. Well, he would, wouldn't he?

I've always had to do Wayne's fighting for him, ever since we were at primary school, and this had gone far enough and I grabbed Mr. Friend's shoulder and went to lay a punch right in the middle of that grinning mask.

And he raised his hand and I felt my fist hit an invisible wall, which yielded like treacle, and he took off his mask and he said two words to me and then he reached across and took Wayne's hand, very gently. . . .

And then the power amp exploded because, like I said, Wayne wasn't very good with connectors and the church hall had electrical wiring that dated back practically to 1800 or something, and then what with the decorations catching fire and everyone screaming and rushing about I didn't really know much about anything until they brought me around in the car park with half my hair burned off and the hall going up like fireworks.

No. I don't know why they haven't found him, either. Not so much as a tooth?

No. I don't know where he is. No, I don't think he owed anyone any money.

(But I think he's got a new job. There's a collector who's got them all—Presley, Hendrix, Lennon, Holly—and he's the only collector who'll ever get a complete collection, anywhere. And Wayne wouldn't pass up a chance like that. Wherever he is now, he's taking them out of their jackets with incredible care and spinning them with love on the turntables of the night. . . .)

Sorry. Talking to myself, there.

I'm just puzzled about one thing. Well, millions of things, actually, but just one thing right at the moment.

I can't imagine why Mr. Friend bothered to wear a mask.

Because he looked just the same underneath, idio— Officer.

What did he say? Well, I daresay he comes to everyone in some sort of familiar way. Perhaps he just wanted to give me a hint. He said, DRIVE SAFELY.

No. No, really. I'll walk home, thanks.

Yes. I'll mind how I go.

The Authors

DOUGLAS HILL writes: "I have mostly been devoted to writing science fiction books, usually in series, like the *Last Legionary* quartet (McElderry/Dell), the *Huntsman* trilogy (McElderry) and the *Colsec* trilogy (McElderry). But more recently I've wanted also to reach readers who prefer the supernatural to outer space. So I've written a 'sword-and-sorcery' *fantasy* adventure, in two books—*Blade of the Poisoner* and *Master of Fiends* (both McElderry)—where four determined people must face an overwhelming host of evil magic and monsters."

TANITH LEE has written a number of books suitable for young adults, including *East of Midnight* (St. Martin's/Ace) and *Dark Castle/White Horse* (Daw).

ROBERT WESTALL writes: "I write too many short stories. For me, a short story is an excuse not to write a novel. I find writing short stories fun; a bit like a game of football or tennis: hard work but soon over. Four days at most. Whereas a novel is like setting out to climb Mount Everest. Four weeks at least; ten years sometimes.

"All my short stories start with a 'What if?' thought. What if two DIY fanatics set out to do-in Count Dracula? What if you meet a *real* Angel? What if you find out you've done everything you've ever meant to do in life, and you don't know what to do next?

"My *funniest* short story was 'The Dracula Tour.' I wrote it in our college library and laughed out loud as I wrote, and all the students thought I was going potty.

"My *saddest* (the only one that makes *me* cry) was 'A Nose Pressed Against Glass.'

"My most *terrible* short story (I don't mean badly written) is 'The Vacancy.' I couldn't *bear* to read that one again.

"My *creepiest* is 'The Creatures in the House.'

"My *happiest* is 'The Girl Who Couldn't Say No.'

"In all, just four volumes of them: *Break of Dark, The Haunting of Chas McGill, Rachel and the Angel* (all Greenwillow), and *Ghosts and Journeys.*"

GARRY KILWORTH has written three books suitable for teenagers. His most recent, *The Foxes of First Dark* (Doubleday), is published as adult fiction.

LISA TUTTLE writes: "The books of mine which I think would be of most interest to young adult readers would be my collection of science fiction short stories, *A Spaceship Built of Stone and Other Stories*—anyone who likes 'The Walled Garden' would almost certainly like some of the stories in that collection. I have another collection in print called *A Nest of Nightmares* (Tor)—those are definitely horror stories, though, and some of them are not for the squeamish! Also of interest might be *Windhaven* (Pocket), a science fiction novel written in collaboration with George R. R. Martin—the main character is a teenager herself during the first section of the book, and the novel (an adventure story set on another planet) is very much concerned with growth and change as experienced both in the lives of individuals and in society as a whole.''

DIANA WYNNE JONES spent her childhood in Essex, a part of the world noted for witches, so it is not surprising that all her stories are about magic. *The Lives of Christopher Chant* (Greenwillow) is her twentieth book for young readers. She won the Guardian Award in 1978 for *Charmed Life* (Greenwillow) and was shortlisted for the Whitbread Award for *Howl's Moving Castle* (Greenwillow), which also won the *Boston Globe/Horn Book* Award. Her other books include *Dogsbody, Fire and Hemlock*, and *Archer's Goon* (all Greenwillow).

MARY RAYNER is best known for her animal fantasies for younger readers, particularly her books about Mr. and Mrs. Pig and their ten irrepressible piglets. She writes, "'The Vision' is the first story I've done specifically for teenagers, but I'd like to do more. It was such a joy to write—for years I had a house full of noise and guitars and young people, and now they've left home, it's suddenly gone quiet and sad.''

GERALDINE HARRIS writes: "The books of mine which I would specifically recommend for teenagers are the *Seven Citadels* series comprising *Prince of the Godborn, The Children of the Wind, The Dead Kingdom* (all Greenwillow/Dell), and *The Seventh Gate* (Greenwillow). These tell a fantasy quest story with a teenage hero and heroine.''

HELEN CRESSWELL doesn't usually write books for teenagers, but the books of hers that she would recommend are *Dear Shrink* (Macmillan) and the seven volumes of *The Bagthorpe Saga: Ordinary Jack, Absolute Zero, Bagthorpes Unlimited, Bagthorpes v. the World, Bagthorpes Abroad, Bagthorpes Haunted* (all Macmillan/Penguin), and *Bagthorpes Liberated* (Macmillan).

EMMA BULL is the author of *War for the Oaks* (Ace), in which a Minneapolis rock musician becomes involved in a fairy civil war. With her husband, Will Shetterly, she wrote "Danceland" for Terri Windling's anthology *Bordertown* (New American Library) and has written short stories for the *Liavek* (Ace) shared-world anthologies, which she and her husband edit.

ROGER ZELAZNY writes: "The only book I've written specifically as a young adult novel is *A Dark Travelling* (Walker), though my humorous science fiction novel *Doorways in the Sand* (Harper) was selected by the American Library Association for its 1976 list of recommended books for young adults. Apart from these, my Amber series has always seemed popular with younger readers. There are ten books in it: *Nine Princes in Amber, The Guns of Avalon, Sign of the Unicorn, The Hand of Oberon,* and *The Courts of Chaos* (all Doubleday/Avon), *Trumps of Doom, Blood of Amber, Sign of Chaos, Knights of Shadows,* and *Frost and Fire* (all Morrow).

TERRY PRATCHETT recommends the Discworld fantasy books, *The Colour of Magic* (St. Martin's) up to *Sourcery* (New American Library) so far. He writes: "They were a lot of fun to write, and I genuinely had no age group in mind; if you can get all the jokes, you're old enough to read them. My mum isn't."